E.C. MADRID

Variant Rising

Contents

After the Fire

Aazar clenched her jaw, focusing on the dish in her hand. The smell of sizzling pork hung in the air, thick and oppressive, a weight pressing down on her chest. It wasn't just the scent; it was the memory of the heat, the burn, the uncontrollable blaze that had once been her power. The meat sizzled, but it was a distant sound compared to the roar in her mind.

"You okay, Z?" Simon's voice broke through the haze, casual but laced with concern. He was busy with the grill, his back to her, unaware of the storm swelling inside her stomach.

Simon was the second-to-last member to join the Order. After his mother passed away from cancer, he wandered the streets alone until Aazar and KJ found him on their way home one day after work. He was one of the many people living in the house shared by discarded Variant teens.

"I'm fine," Aazar muttered, the words barely audible, her voice a thin mask. She scrubbed at the dish, but it did nothing to stop the nausea.

Simon glanced over his shoulder, his brows knitting together. "You sure? I can open a window."

"No, I'm fine," she repeated in a lighter tone. "I'm almost done anyway."

He hesitated, then shrugged and returned to his cooking, oblivious to the way the sound of the sizzling meat seemed to sync with the erratic thumping in her chest. It wasn't just the smell. It was everything that came with it: the memories, the screams, the burning heat of her powers. Her hand tightened around the dish, her fingers stiff and cold against the smooth surface.

She took a deep breath, but it didn't help. It never did. The ghosts of the past lingered. She dried the plate and set it on the rack, her breath shallow. She didn't linger and ran into the hallway.

But her escape was short-lived.

"Hey, Z!" Logan's voice rang out, high and bright, and she almost cringed at the unexpected energy. He wasn't much younger than her, but his small stature made him seem fragile.

"Check this out!" he shouted, excitement pulling at every inch of his frame.

She turned just in time to see him squint his eyes and focus on his finger before it wavered and disappeared from view, like a mirage.

"You did it!" Her voice cracked a little. "How did you: "

Logan's grin was wide, unabashed. "I stayed up last night practicing. Channeling, focusing... I think I've got it now."

Logan was the last member to join the group and was just getting control over his powers. Invisibility seemed to take more physical energy to use than she'd realized before. Aazar never thought of herself as a mentor, but she found herself in the role regardless.

"That's really draining, Logan," she said, the words falling out before she could stop herself from nagging. "You shouldn't: "

"I know, but once I figured it out, I couldn't stop!" he interrupted, his voice high, excited. The kind of excitement that only the young could possess, the hope of being on the verge of something new, something better.

She hid the worry on her face by forcing a smile. Let him have this moment. He deserves it.

"Say it!" Logan pleaded, bouncing from foot to foot. "Just say you're proud!"

Aazar looked around the room, pretending to consider it. Finally, she leaned in, her voice dropping to a whisper.

"I'm proud."

The cheer that followed was pure, untainted. Logan darted past her, his hoots and hollers trailing behind him, but Aazar stood still, letting the moment wash over her without truly letting it in.

The house she and KJ had built was a product of years of hard labor. The first year had been grueling: KJ working in the fisheries, and Aazar doing laundry for the wealthy residents who lived in the mega-pods by the sea. The work was hard, but they'd saved every penny, and after a year of grinding, they'd built this small, modest house and filled it with new friends.

As she adjusted to life on the California Islands, she had found a new peace in simplicity. The days were busy but clear, and she found her purpose in teaching the other Variants, offering lessons on Flenoid's technique. They'd never planned to house so many, but when people showed up at their door, asking for shelter and guidance, they didn't turn anyone away. Now, their home was full, with more coming every weekend.

Aazar had never thought she'd be good at teaching. But the way the others looked to her for answers, for calm, it had become her new role. Not because she was naturally serene but because it was the only way to keep herself from losing control.

The house felt smaller now, as if it had been shrinking ever since they'd moved in. The kitchen was too tight, the walls too close, and the air, thick with the smell of pork, felt like it was closing in on her.

KJ's hands came around her waist from behind, warm and solid, pulling her back to the present. His chest against her back steadied her, and she felt the slow exhale of his breath against her skin.

"Brooding in the hallway solves nothing," KJ murmured, his voice like a thread pulling her from the depths.

Aazar couldn't stop the sigh that escaped her lips. "Sorry."

He gently swayed her side to side, his chin resting on her shoulder. "We're moving forward, remember?"

Her jaw tightened, but she nodded, biting down on the lump rising in her throat.

Aazar found herself more anxious since leaving The Order. Although she hadn't lost control of her powers in a while, she felt like she had lost her ability to go with the flow of things. She was often overwhelmed by memories and thoughts, never truly feeling comfortable in the present.

KJ squeezed her tighter. "I love you," he whispered.

The words landed like an anchor, sinking deep into her chest. She turned in his arms, wrapping her arms around his neck. "I love you too."

He kissed her softly, his lips steady and sure, and for a moment, she let herself dissolve into him, letting go of everything but the feel of him against her, the warm safety of this life.

But as the kiss broke, KJ pulled back just enough to catch her eyes, his gaze filled with understanding.

"Come on," he said, his voice a little firmer now, though still kind. "Everyone's waiting."

His hands slid from her waist to her shoulders, and he turned her gently toward the living room, giving her one last squeeze. "Deep breaths," he smiled, his touch light and reassuring. "I've got you."

She nodded, and together, they stepped into the room where the others were gathered. The air was filled with the hum of casual chatter, of young faces lounging on pull-out couches, of the smell of cheap beer and sweat.

"Finally!" Hugo called out, leaping to his feet, his voice high with impatience. "We can get going!"

Hugo had the hardest time making friends in the new group. He often made jokes about things that most people didn't find funny, and his power to disrupt electronic signals didn't make him many friends when he lost control of it. Hugo crossed his arms.

"Where's Simon?" he asked, his brow furrowing.

"He's in the kitchen," Aazar answered, before Simon appeared in the hallway, sandwich in hand, chewing absently.

"I wanted to eat first," Simon mumbled between bites, avoiding Hugo's hostile gaze. "Bar food's expensive."

Hugo let out a frustrated groan. "We were supposed to leave ten minutes ago!"

Aazar had learned, in the months that followed their escape from The Order, that different stress triggers often ignited powers. Hugo lost control of his powers when he became overwhelmed. For KJ, it was guilt. For her, it was anger. For Lizzie, Aazar suspected it was happiness, though she preferred not to think about Lizzie.

"We can leave now," Aazar said, her voice steady, trying to push things forward. "Simon, you can finish it in the car."

Simon swallowed the last bite and grinned. "I'm already done!"

Hugo groaned again, but the rest of the group seemed unfazed, their energy light and eager.

Simon wiped his mouth on his sleeve, grinning wide. "Let's get drunk!"

The others cheered, and Aazar forced a smile. She wished she could feel the excitement, but all she felt was the dull ache of something missing, something lost. Ever since the incident with the Belizes, she hadn't laughed like she used to. Everything felt... muted, as if a part of her had been taken.

KJ's hand squeezed hers again, a soft understanding in his smile. "It'll be fun," he said, his words steady.

Aazar returned the smile for him, though it felt more like a mask. "I know."

Fault Lines

The California coast felt like a soft embrace around Aazar as she stepped out of the van, the cool night air clinging to her skin. Her boots met the cracked pavement of the dive bar's parking lot, the asphalt worn down by time and use, just like everything else in this place. The Rusty Anchor: a name that felt worn and old even before she set foot here: stood between two neon-lit convenience stores that screamed cheap and quick. The sign above flickered erratically, its glow fading in and out like it had just enough life to keep going. But it suited the place. It wasn't meant to shine. It was meant to hide the wear and tear of a hundred stories: too many to count.

"Let's just have a drink, relax for once," KJ's voice was low, the words almost lost in the buzz of chatter and clinking glasses coming from inside.

Aazar nodded, grateful, and blinked a few times. She was still getting used to the brown contacts she wore when she went out to hide the red in her eyes. She could feel the tension pulling at her, but she tried to ignore it. She didn't need to think about the past tonight. Not with KJ by her side.

The door creaked as they entered, and the smell of stale beer, smoke, and cheap whiskey wrapped around her like an old coat. The air was thick with it, hanging in a haze that made the dim interior seem even darker. This wasn't the kind of place that pretended to be something it wasn't. No polished floors or clean-cut smiles here. The walls were lined with age and regret, the jukebox in the corner filling the space with soft music, but it was the murmur of voices and the clink of bottles that carried the real rhythm of the bar.

The hum of chatter felt like an ocean crashing against Aazar's chest. Every word, every clink of a glass, the scratchy music in the corner, all of it swirled together in a blur. But KJ's steady presence beside her, his hand brushing hers as he leaned in, grounded her like a lifeline in a storm.

Aazar's pulse slowed, the familiar noise, the chaos of it all, seeping into her veins. This was where people came to forget, to lose themselves in the noise, in the anonymity. She took a deep breath, letting it fill her chest, a fleeting sense of normalcy washing over her. For tonight, she could pretend to be like everyone else. Just a face in the crowd.

They found a corner booth. Simon and Logan had already started talking to a few of the regulars, the kind of people who lived here, who called places like this home. Aazar watched Logan, his once-shaky control over his powers now turning into something more solid, more assured. She caught him showing off, just a flicker of power, a small, controlled display, and it made something warm stir in her chest. He was getting stronger.

But it wasn't enough to chase away the darkness that lingered in her mind. Her eyes darted around the bar, half-listening to the conversations around her, but her mind stayed elsewhere. Peter would have loved this place. The guilt, that sharp, familiar ache, crept up again, clinging to her like a shadow she couldn't shake.

The noise around her seemed to fade until a raised voice cut through the haze.

At the far end of the bar, two men stood. Their sharp suits looked out of place, too polished for the grit of this place. The way they carried themselves, all confidence and entitlement, made them stand out. The shorter man with dark black hair and blue eyes kept his voice low, but it was filled with something cold and demanding.

"Say that again…Go on." His words cut through the noise like a blade.

The taller one, with blonde hair and dark brown eyes, tried to calm the first one down, his hands raised in a placating gesture. "Johnny, not here. Not with these people."

But Johnny wasn't listening. He was already stepping forward, his eyes dark with something that Aazar didn't like, didn't trust. He was close now, right in the face of a man who was too drunk to understand what was happening.

"Just walk away, man," the drunk man slurred, trying to push Johnny away with a weak shove. "I don't want any trouble."

Johnny didn't seem to care. "I don't care what you want," he spat, his fists tightening at his sides. "Repeat what you said."

Aazar's body tensed. It wasn't the first fight she'd seen in a bar, but there was something about Johnny's arrogance, the way his posture screamed entitlement, that made her blood run cold.

As Johnny's voice rose, so did the heat in her chest; an instinctive, dangerous reaction that she had long since learned to hold down. It was a struggle, and it made her jaw clench even harder. She couldn't let it out. Not now. Not here. She had to be in control. She had to prove she was more than the fire that once burned everything in its path.

KJ noticed the change in her energy. His eyes narrowed, his posture shifting as he watched the fight across the room.

The tension in the air thickened. Johnny shoved the drunk man backward, sending him stumbling into a table. Glasses shattered, the noise loud against the stillness that followed. A few patrons stood up, taking cautious steps back, eyes flicking nervously between the fight and the bar's exit. Aazar stood, her body moving before her mind could catch up. She wouldn't let this go on.

Without hesitation, she crossed the room, her steps deliberate, firm. KJ's gaze followed, but he didn't move. He knew she could handle this.

The drunk man on the ground tried to stand, his eyes darting back and forth at the appalled faces in the bar. Johnny had his fists up now, his face red, breathing hard with rage. Johnny's companion was trying to pull him back, but it wasn't working. Aazar stepped between them, calm but commanding.

"That's enough," she said, her voice steady as she locked eyes with Johnny.

Johnny faltered, just for a moment. The tall man's gaze flicked between the two of them, surprised by the calm in Aazar's voice.

Johnny exhaled sharply, his hands falling to his sides, but the tension didn't dissipate. "I don't take orders from anyone," he muttered, his voice sharp and defiant.

Aazar's eyes remained fixed on him, unwavering. "Then consider this a warning," she said, her voice firm and unyielding. "You should back off."

Johnny's jaw tightened, his face twisted in frustration. But after a moment, he turned on his heel and stormed toward the back of the bar, his companion following behind him, throwing Aazar a look full of disbelief and something else: admiration, maybe.

The air in the bar shifted again, and the energy returned to normal as patrons resumed their conversations. Aazar walked back to the booth, the adrenaline still buzzing through her veins, but she kept her movements slow and deliberate.

KJ was waiting for her, his brow furrowed, his eyes studying her.

"You okay?" he asked, his voice low, careful.

Aazar smiled tightly, the edges of it pulling at the corners of her mouth. "Yeah. Just a little annoyance handled."

She sat down beside him, but her eyes flicked back to Johnny and his tall companion, who were seated in a corner, their eyes still fixed on her.

After a few moments, Johnny stood, the tall man following behind. Their footsteps were light, purposeful, and Aazar couldn't help the way her body stiffened, a quick flash of wariness rushing through her. She couldn't be caught off guard, not here.

"Hey," Johnny said, his voice smoother now, his challenge replaced by something more calculated. "I lost myself back there. I apologize." He put his hand out for a handshake. "I'm Johnny. This is Caleb."

Caleb stepped forward with a million dollar grin and held his hand out for a handshake. Johnny stepped behind the man, happy to be done with his apology.

Aazar raised an eyebrow, her gaze cool as she sized Caleb up, he was a blonde with brown eyes and a lanky demeanor. "Hey," she said, her voice clipped, not giving her own name.

Johnny, standing slightly behind Caleb, shifted uncomfortably, his eyes darting between them.

"We're just trying to make peace," Caleb muttered as he shot a glare towards Johnny.

Johnny rolled his eyes, but Caleb ignored it. He turned his attention fully to Aazar.

"How about a drink?" he asked, his smile widening. "We're here to relax. You seem like someone who knows how to handle herself. Someone good to know."

Aazar hesitated, the instinct to push them away clawing at her. But Caleb's challenge, the way his gaze didn't waver, piqued something in her. She glanced at KJ, who was watching the scene intently, his eyes sharp but unreadable. She gave him a quick nod, reassuring him. He didn't look happy, but he relaxed slightly.

Aazar sighed. "Alright. One drink."

Caleb's grin widened, Johnny's eyebrows shot up in surprise. "Great. Come on, we'll make sure you enjoy it."

They led her to a corner booth, Caleb flagging down the bartender and ordering whiskey. The drinks arrived, and Caleb leaned in slightly, his voice smooth, almost too smooth. "So, tell me about yourself," he said, his words casual but laced with something sharper. "Where are you from? You don't look like you're from around here."

Aazar sipped her drink, careful to maintain a neutral expression. "I'm from Arizona," she said, her voice even, the details vague enough to keep him guessing.

Caleb raised an eyebrow, his interest piqued. "Arizona, huh? Interesting. I've been there a few times. Lovely place. You ever think about going back?"

Aazar didn't answer right away. Johnny's eyes flicked nervously to Aazar, his hands twitching at his sides. His discomfort was clear, his gaze shifting between her and his friend, but she wasn't sure why.

"I haven't really thought about it," Aazar said, setting her glass down. "I like it here."

Caleb nodded and glanced at Johnny, who kept his face neutral.

"You got a name?"

"I'm called 'Z'"

"'Z'?" he asked with his eyebrows raised, "Just a letter? How mysterious."

Aazar took a sip of her drink and didn't answer.

Caleb's eyes narrowed just a fraction, and she could feel the shift in his posture. "I've been looking for a new bodyguard," he said, his tone dropping to something more confidential, more enticing. "My last guy retired, and I need someone who can handle themselves. I think you've got the look for the job."

Aazar didn't miss a beat. "Bodyguard?" she asked, her interest flickering despite herself. This conversation had shifted into dangerous territory, but something about the offer pulled at her. The fishery wasn't bringing in as much money as she'd hoped, and doing odd jobs wasn't cutting it.

"Why me?" Aazar asked.

"What do you mean?"

"I mean, I weigh 129 pounds dripping wet." She said. "Shouldn't you look for someone with bigger? With more muscle?"

"I have a feeling there's more to you than you're letting on," Caleb said, leaning back in his chair, his confidence unshaken. "I've got some things going on. I need someone who can handle a little danger and isn't afraid to step in when necessary. Judging from what I just saw, I think you'd be perfect. What do you say?"

Aazar thought about it for a moment, her gaze flicking to the booth, where KJ was still watching. The idea was tempting. Aazar could feel it, the lure of the job. Power. Control. It wasn't the kind of life she wanted, but something about Caleb's challenge twisted at her, calling to the part of her that still burned with the need to assert her dominance. But she wasn't that person anymore. She wasn't supposed to be.

"I'll think about it," she said, her voice noncommittal.

Caleb didn't seem put off. If anything, he enjoyed the challenge. "Take your time," he said, his smile wide and knowing. He slid her a white card with a QR code on it. "Make an appointment when you're ready."

Aazar nodded, "I'm going to head back to my group."

"No worries," Caleb grinned again. "I know I'll be seeing you soon."

Aazar walked back to the booth, where KJ looked worried.

"What was that about?" KJ asked.

"He wanted to give me a job."

"A job," KJ perked up, "We could use something more steady."

Aazar nodded and looked back at the rich men at the table in the back. Caleb threw his head back in laughter at a quiet joke Johnny must have cracked. She wasn't sure if she could trust them, but she wasn't sure that she had a choice.

Terms of Power

Aazar stepped out of the car, the cool ocean breeze tugging at her jacket as she took in the towering office building before her. Caleb's office had been described to her over the phone as "modern" and "exclusive," but those words didn't quite capture the sense of overwhelming wealth she felt standing in its shadow. The building was a massive monolith of glass and steel, gleaming under the afternoon sun like it had been designed to reflect the affluence of its occupants: cold and flawless. A thing built to impress.

She exhaled slowly, trying to push aside the creeping unease that always tightened its grip whenever she stepped into a world that felt so foreign. This was Caleb's world, not hers. She imagined Norma would be drooling at the chance to work in an office space like this. Norma would fit in perfectly. But Aazar wasn't Norma.

A frown tugged at her lips at the thought of her old colleague, but she quickly shook it off. *Focus.* She had an interview to prepare for, and it was better to keep her mind on that. The money and luxury were worlds away from the life she knew, but the offer… it was hard to resist. A real security job. A chance to get paid for something she was actually good at.

The automatic doors slid open with a soft swish, and she stepped inside. The lobby took her breath away: not for its opulence, but for its stark simplicity. Wide glass windows flooded the space with natural light, revealing sleek furniture and polished marble floors that reflected the elegance of the place. A receptionist sat behind a minimalist desk, her fingers tapping absentmindedly on a keyboard.

"Can I help you?" the woman asked, smiling politely.

"I'm here to meet Caleb," Aazar said, keeping her tone casual, though her nerves were starting to show. "I'm Z. He should be expecting me."

The receptionist checked her computer, nodding as she stood up. "Mr. Caleb is waiting for you. Please follow me."

Aazar followed her down the hallway toward the elevator, trying not to feel like an intruder. The elevator assistant pressed a button for her and ushered her inside. The doors closed with barely a sound, and the elevator began its ascent. The building stretched upward, and the sudden height made Aazar's stomach churn. For a moment, the vertigo took over, and she felt like a speck in a world so much larger than herself.

When the elevator doors opened, she was greeted by another assistant who directed her down a long hallway. The view of the ocean stretched out in front of her, as pristine and perfect as a postcard. The sound of the waves crashing against the shore was distant, almost surreal. Aazar's footsteps echoed in the silence of the building, the space so vast that it swallowed up any trace of noise.

The assistant stopped in front of an office door, knocked lightly, and then opened it. "Mr. Caleb, Ms. Z is here."

"Send her in," a voice called from inside, smooth and confident.

Aazar stepped inside, her gaze sweeping over the room. It was exactly what she expected: polished, sleek, and modern. Large abstract art adorned the walls, and the floors were a glossy wood that gleamed under the soft lighting. Behind a massive desk sat Caleb, looking relaxed but commanding. He looked up as she entered, his expression shifting from casual to calculated as he studied her.

"Z," Caleb greeted her, rising from his chair with a smile. "Thanks for coming in."

Aazar returned the smile, though it felt stiff on her face. She kept her eyes on the room around her: the luxury, the pristine perfection of it all. She reminded herself that this was just an interview. Nothing more. She had a job to do.

"Please, take a seat," Caleb gestured to the chair across from him, his voice smooth and welcoming.

She sat down, crossing her legs and folding her hands in her lap, trying to hide the slight tremor in her fingers. The calm exterior was all she had left to control herself.

"You make your assistants call you 'Mr. Caleb'?" Aazar asked, forcing a nervous smile to break the ice.

Caleb chuckled softly, easing the tension in the room. "No one ever mentions that! I think last names are overrated, and I don't want to be confused with my dad. I thought you'd understand 'Z.'"

Aazar's eyes flicked downward, not because she felt small, but because she didn't want him to see how much his words affected her. He leaned back in his chair, his hands steepled together as he regarded her with a keen, assessing gaze.

"I'm going to get right to the point, Z," he said, his voice dropping an octave. "I need someone who knows what they're doing. Someone who's seen the kind of situations I deal with. And you..." He studied her for a moment longer, as if weighing something hidden beneath the surface. "You seem like you've got experience."

Aazar's lips parted, but she didn't speak. She wasn't about to confirm or deny his assumptions, but she knew he was right. She had seen more than her fair share of danger. She just didn't talk about it.

Caleb leaned forward slightly, his voice lowering. "I work in a business where people make enemies: real enemies. I'm trying to create a peaceful world through innovative technology, but there are a lot of people who don't like the project I'm spearheading, and they'll do anything to stop me. I'm a little like Bryce Wayne in that regard. You know, a rich, attractive playboy millionaire trying to save the world from scum of the earth."

He chuckled at his own joke, but Aazar didn't respond. Instead, she kept her eyes fixed on him, waiting.

"I've got security, but frankly, they're too green. Too inexperienced. I need someone who can protect me when things get ugly. I need someone who can handle the worst situations without hesitation."

Aazar's mind raced, but her face remained neutral. She had dealt with her own brand of danger. This wasn't a world she was used to, but it wasn't unfamiliar either. And at least she'd be getting paid for it.

"You're offering me a job as your security?" she asked, her voice steady but with an undercurrent of curiosity.

Caleb's smile deepened, his gaze never wavering. "Exactly. And I think you fit the bill."

"Why?" Aazar said. "I just stopped a bar fight. I might not even be able to protect you."

"No one walks in between three men calmly without being able to handle themselves. I think it would take people off guard." Caleb said. "Plus, it was fascinating to witness. I'd like to see more of it."

Aazar leaned back in her chair, crossing her arms as the weight of the offer settled on her. She let the silence stretch between them for a moment before speaking again. "What's the catch?"

Caleb's eyes gleamed with something darker. "No catch. But let me be clear. This isn't your average job. You'll be protecting me from people who want to see me fall. People who will stop at nothing to make that happen. And the job will require more than just standing by my side. You'll need to be alert and anticipate threats before they happen. It's not for the faint of heart."

He waited for her to comment, but she didn't say anything.

Caleb continued. "You'll make $200,000 a year," he said, his tone flat and businesslike. "More if you prove yourself. And I'm not one for short-term arrangements. If we work well together, this could be a long-term position."

Aazar's heart skipped a beat at the number. Two hundred thousand. It was more money than she'd ever seen in one place. More than she ever thought she'd make in her lifetime. The idea of security, a steady income: it was tempting. But at what cost?

"Well..." She hesitated, her voice quieter now, laced with skepticism.

Caleb's smile thinned slightly, but there was no hesitation in his voice. "I don't need someone who's going to freeze when it counts. I need someone who can act without hesitation. You've got that edge." He studied her, eyes running over her form, measuring. "Plus, no one will see you coming. They'll probably think I'm dating you."

Aazar didn't respond immediately. She could feel the weight of his words, but she wasn't ready to let him read her so easily. He wanted to challenge her. To see if she'd bite. But she wasn't in the mood to play games.

She sat back, her gaze drifting to the ocean outside. The waves crashed relentlessly, each one a reminder of the decisions she faced. The money was tempting, but the world Caleb lived in: the dangers, the high-stakes game…it wasn't her world. Not yet.

"I want an open-ended contract," Aazar demanded. "I know you want someone long term, and I'm willing to do that, but I want to be able to quit at a moment's notice if this job gets too dangerous. I have people I need to protect."

Caleb nodded solemnly. "That can be arranged, but in return, I would like to be able to fire you at any time as well."

Aazar thought about it for a few more seconds.

"I'll do it," she said finally, her voice steady, the resolve settling into her bones.

Caleb's smile returned, warmer now. "Good. I'll have Cindy draw up the paperwork." He leaned back in his chair, his hands behind his head as he relaxed. "I knew you'd see things my way. You start tomorrow."

Aazar nodded, her decision made. As she stood to leave, she noticed Johnny stepping into the office. His eyes flicked to her, and for a brief moment, they locked. In that instant, she saw something in his expression: discomfort, perhaps, or disapproval. Whatever it was, it was gone too quickly for her to pinpoint.

Johnny gave her a polite smile before turning his attention to Caleb, who greeted him warmly.

"Johnny," Caleb said, his smile wide and welcoming. "What's up?"

Aazar stepped past them, her mind already racing with the implications of the decision she'd just made. Johnny's gaze lingered on her, but she didn't let it stop her. This was her choice. And now, she'd have to live with it.

Bodyguard

The drive back to the house was quiet. The sun had begun to dip below the horizon, casting an orange glow that seemed to stretch across the sky forever. Aazar felt the weight of the decision she'd made earlier settle deep into her chest, pressing on her like a heavy stone. She hadn't been prepared for the unease that followed her after agreeing to Caleb's job. The thought of stepping into his world, with all its high stakes and smooth talk, unsettled her more than she cared to admit.

He had been vague about what he actually did for work. Caleb said he was saving the world, but he wouldn't be the first person who had said that and been up to horrible things. Believing Avery was a good guy got her into a lot of trouble, and she didn't like the idea of helping with something she didn't agree with. She needed to find out exactly what he was doing soon.

KJ drove the car home with his hands tight on the steering wheel. His was body tense in the way it always was when something was on his mind. She could feel the unspoken question between them, a pressure in the air that made the silence heavier than it should be.

"So, are you feeling good about the job?" KJ asked, his voice steady but with a subtle edge that told her more than the words did.

Aazar glanced over at him, her hand resting in her lap, trying to gauge his mood. She didn't want to lie, but she didn't want to drag him into this unease either. "Yeah," she said slowly, her tone more uncertain than she intended. "I think it's the right move. It's solid work. Caleb knows what he's doing, and the money's too good to pass up."

KJ nodded but didn't speak right away. He was quiet, thoughtful, his fingers still gripping the steering wheel as they drove. She could tell that this job, this whole situation, was making him uncomfortable. It was more than just the job itself: it was the kind of world Caleb operated in. A world KJ knew well enough to be wary of.

"You're not worried about the people you'll be dealing with?" KJ's question hung in the air, and she could hear the unspoken concern in his voice.

"I thought you wanted me to take the job," Aazar said.

"I do!" KJ said quickly, "I mean I did. When I thought it was an office job. I don't know how I feel about you working security. It could get dangerous."

Aazar hesitated. The thought had crossed her mind, of course. Caleb reminded her of Avery in so many ways: smooth-talking, persistent, with a smile that could charm anyone into doing whatever he wanted. But she couldn't bring herself to mention Avery, not to KJ. She still wasn't sure how to handle that part of her past, especially now that things with KJ were so new, so fragile. It was still too raw.

"I'll be fine," she said, giving him a smile that she hoped looked more confident than she felt. "I know how to handle myself. It's not like I'm new to this, KJ. I can handle it."

"I know you can," KJ said softly, his voice full of something unspoken. "But I just want you to be careful."

The rest of the drive passed in a blur. Aazar's mind churned with the weight of her decision: the job, the potential danger, and the shadow of Avery still lingering in the back of her thoughts. Would he be surprised by her choice? She didn't think so. Avery knew her better than anyone, knew what she was capable of and what she had to do to survive. But then, she shook her head. No. Avery made her think he knew her. He hadn't really known her at all.

When they arrived home, the evening seemed to slow. KJ was still quiet, his worry hanging in the air between them. But for once, he didn't push her. Instead, they settled into the evening in a shared silence. The sound of the ocean crashing against the shore and the loud chatter of their roommates filled the spaces between them.

Later, in the privacy of their bedroom, Aazar lay awake, the rush of thoughts racing through her mind like an unrelenting current. KJ's warm body pressed against hers was the only thing that grounded her in the present. His steady breathing, the rise and fall of his chest, was a comfort, a reminder that she wasn't alone in this.

"KJ?" she whispered into the dark, breaking the silence between them.

He stirred beside her, his voice thick with sleep. "Yeah?"

"I'm worried," Aazar admitted, the words coming out barely louder than a breath. "Not about the job, but about myself. I'm worried that I'll lose control. That something will happen, and I won't be able to stop it."

KJ shifted, his hand gently cupping her face, his thumb brushing over her skin with slow, soothing movements. "Aazar, you haven't lost control of your powers in almost two years. You've learned to handle them. You've come so far."

"I know," she said, her voice trembling as she fought to keep it steady. "But what if I can't keep it together? What if something happens while I'm on the job? What if I hurt someone?"

KJ pulled her closer, his warmth enveloping her like a shield. "You're not the person you used to be, Aazar. You've changed. You're stronger now. You're not going to lose control. Not now."

She closed her eyes, letting the comfort of his words wash over her, even as doubt gnawed at the edges of her mind. She needed to believe him. She wanted to trust him completely, but the uncertainty still lingered, like a shadow at the edges of her thoughts.

"You've got this," KJ murmured, pressing a soft kiss to her forehead. "And if you ever feel like you're losing yourself, I'll be right here, holding you together."

Aazar nodded. With KJ by her side, she could face anything. The fear, the doubt: they were just temporary things. She could handle it. With him, she could handle anything.

Aazar's thoughts began to quiet, and before long, she drifted into a peaceful sleep in KJ's arms.

* * *

The next morning, Aazar found herself in the back of a sleek limo, the plush interior cocooning her in quiet luxury. Caleb's meetings had gone smoothly: no drama, no issues. From what she could tell, he was in negotiations with the Mafia to buy computer components, but she wasn't sure what he was building. Whatever it was couldn't be above board if he held meetings in the back of storage rooms and parlors. Caleb was on a call as he looked out of the window.

"Yeah, tell him the deal's on," Caleb said into his earpiece, his tone relaxed, professional. "Just make sure you call Cindy with the details."

He disconnected the call with a sigh. "Finally!" he exclaimed, tossing the earpiece onto the seat beside him. "That was the last stop. You want a drink?"

He gestured at the decanter sitting in the armrest. Aazar glanced at it, but she shook her head. She wasn't in the mood.

He shrugged, pouring himself a generous glass. "Suit yourself."

Aazar gazed out the window as the cityscape blurred past. Caleb didn't have a drinking problem per se, but she wasn't sure she'd ever seen him sober. He didn't seem drunk, but there was something about the way he held himself. He was always just a little detached from the world around him.

"So," Caleb said as he took a sip of his drink, "Tell me about yourself. Do you have a family?"

"I have friends," Aazar said shortly.

"Do you have a boyfriend or..."

"Yes," Aazar said. "We've been together for a little while."

"Are you faithful?" Caleb asked.

Aazar glared.

"I'm kidding," He said with his hands up, "I'm just kidding."

Aazar gave him a grimace. Caleb had been subtly hitting on her all day, and she wasn't a fan of it. She wondered if that was really the reason he gave her the job.

"You have to lighten up, Z," Caleb said, spilling a little bit of his drink. "You've made it! No more struggling, no more odd jobs. You should take a load off."

"You're not paying me to relax, Caleb."

Caleb rolled his eyes and went back to his drink.

The limo turned sharply into a narrow alley, and the streetlights cast long, looming shadows on the pavement. The car jerked to a stop. The driver's voice came through the intercom. "Sorry, we're having some issues. Please give me a moment."

Aazar's heart rate quickened. Something was wrong. She felt it, deep in her bones. She glanced at Caleb, who was relaxed, too relaxed, as if nothing were amiss. But the tension in the air was palpable, and Aazar couldn't shake the feeling that things were about to take a turn.

Then, the door on her side of the limo was yanked open. A Variant, clad in black, stood in the doorway, their face hidden behind a dark mask. Aazar barely had time to react before the air crackled with the surge of electricity.

Caleb dove out of the way, but the Variant's hand shot forward, sending a burst of crackling power straight toward her.

Without thinking, Aazar's instincts took over. Flames erupted from her hand, a searing blast that shot toward the attacker. Her aim was precise, and the fireball hit its target, sending the Variant stumbling back, the force of the blast knocking them to the ground.

The Variant twitched on the pavement, their body convulsing from the shock of the fire, before finally going still.

Aazar leaped from the limo, rushing to the downed figure. Her heart was pounding, and adrenaline rushed through her veins. She crouched to examine the Variant, her mind still spinning from the sudden attack.

"Please don't be dead," Aazar begged in a quiet voice. "Don't be dead…"

She didn't want to be a murderer again.

Caleb stepped out of the limo without hesitation, slow claps echoing in the tense silence. "Wow, Fire! I knew your power would be amazing, but fire? I would've never guessed."

Aazar froze, her hand still smoking from the fireball she'd just released. She turned sharply, her eyes narrowing at Caleb. He wasn't shocked. Not at all. If anything, he looked… impressed.

"You knew?" Aazar's voice was tight, disbelief clouding her words.

Caleb flashed a knowing smile, his eyes gleaming with something unreadable. "Of course, I knew. I'm a Variant too. I was hoping you'd get a chance to show me what you've got, and boy, did you deliver!"

Aazar's breath caught in her throat. Caleb knew? Had he known from the beginning? Her thoughts raced, the implications hitting her hard.

"How could you-"

Caleb interrupted, his tone casual, almost playful. "We'll talk about it over a drink. There's a dive bar I want to check out. I'll have Johnny meet us there."

Aazar blinked, still processing. "You mean Johnny-"

"All will be revealed at the bar," Caleb said with a grin, adopting a mock mystical tone. He stepped back into the limo, his posture confident, as if this moment were no surprise to him.

Aazar stared at the unconscious Variant in front of her, her pulse hammering in her ears. She couldn't shake the feeling that everything she thought she knew about Caleb and this entire situation had just shifted. As if on autopilot, she reached down and yanked the assailant's jacket, pulling out a crumpled photo that had slipped from his pocket.

She unfolded it quickly. Her eyes widened in shock. The photo was of her: of Aazar, her face unmistakable, but there was something more. On the back, written in a familiar scrawl, was her full name. Beneath it, a date and a short sentence: "Handle it."

Aazar's breath hitched. She recognized the handwriting instantly.

Avery's handwriting.

The realization slammed into her like a punch to the gut. This wasn't a random attack. It was deliberate. The Variant hadn't been after just anyone: they'd been after her. And Avery had orchestrated it.

Her heart raced as she shoved the photo into her pocket, trying to quell the wave of nausea threatening to rise in her throat. She stood up, her mind spinning as the truth settled heavily in her chest.

This was no coincidence. This was a message, a deliberate move.

Without another word, Aazar climbed back into the limo. The door slammed shut behind her, and she sat in the plush interior, her hand still clenched around the photo.

Her mind raced as the limo pulled away, the city lights flashing by, but she could hardly see them. All she could think of was the photo. And the question that now hung in the air: Why after all of this time?

Invisible Costs

azar sat in the plush velvet seat of the VIP lounge, the dim lighting casting soft, intimate shadows across the faces of the well-dressed patrons around her. Caleb and Johnny were across from her in a private booth, sipping their drinks. Their conversation was light and casual, but Aazar couldn't shake the feeling that something was lurking beneath the surface: something she hadn't yet figured out.

The hum of the lounge, the clink of glasses, and the low murmur of conversation felt distant as her thoughts drifted. Her phone buzzed in her pocket, cutting through her distracted focus. She glanced at the screen: KJ. A tightness gripped her chest at the thought of the call.

Excusing herself, she stood up and moved toward a quieter corner, her fingers brushing against the cold glass of the wall as she stepped away from the booth.

When she answered, KJ's voice was warm but thick with sleep. "Hey, I just woke up and realized you're still not home. What's up?"

Aazar leaned against the wall, her gaze darting across the crowded lounge as she tried to steady herself. " I'm in a lounge with my boss. KJ, I need to talk to you about something."

His tone shifted instantly, picking up on the tension in her voice. "What's going on? You sound… off. Are you okay?"

She exhaled. Her eyes dropped to the ground as she searched for the right way to explain. "Something happened tonight. We were attacked. Me and Caleb."

There was a long pause, silence filling the space between them. KJ's voice came back, thick with concern. "Attacked? What happened? Are you alright?"

"I'm fine," she said quickly, her voice betraying her with the slightest tremor. "But it wasn't random. We were ambushed. Someone with electrical powers. They knew exactly where we'd be. It felt like they were waiting for us."

KJ's voice grew tight. "Who did it? Do you know who it was?"

Aazar rubbed her temples, not wanting to mention Avery's handwriting. The frustration built as she tried to piece the situation together. "Not exactly. But… I think it was someone from The Order."

The silence on the other end of the line was sharp, and Aazar could hear KJ's breath catch. "The Order?" he repeated, his voice darkening. "You think they sent someone after you?"

"I don't know for sure, but it makes sense," Aazar said, the heaviness of it all sinking deeper. "They've grown a lot in the last few years, KJ. They've got resources. I found a photo on the attacker. My name was on the back, with a date."

"Shit," KJ swore softly. "Aazar, this is serious. You shouldn't be out there. We need to leave. We need to go somewhere safe."

Aazar's chest tightened at the thought. "And run? Again? You know I'm not doing that. I'm done with that life. I'm not hiding anymore."

"I know," KJ's voice softened, but the concern was still there. "But you can't keep doing this by yourself."

"I know," she cut him off gently. "But I don't want to put you in danger. You've been through enough."

"Stop," KJ interjected, his voice tender but firm. "We've been through worse. I'm with you. No matter what."

Aazar smiled faintly, the tension in her shoulders easing just a fraction. "I don't know what I'd do without you, KJ."

He chuckled softly, his warmth filling the silence between them. "I'll be here, Aazar. Always."

The comfort in his words was more than she could articulate. She stayed on the line with him a few moments longer, just letting the quiet between them settle in, the steady rhythm of his breathing a reminder that she wasn't alone.

"I'll be careful, KJ," she said finally, her voice resolute. "I promise."

He sighed, lighter now, like the weight had lifted off his chest too. "I know you will. Just… stay safe, okay?"

"I will," she reassured him before hanging up.

Aazar tucked her phone back into her pocket, a new sense of resolve hardening within her. The conversation had calmed her, but what had just happened still shook her. She needed to focus on her new boss and figure out what Caleb's world was really about.

When she returned to the booth, Caleb greeted her with an easy smile, swirling the amber liquid in his glass as Johnny's gaze lingered on her, his expression unreadable.

"Everything alright?" Caleb asked, raising an eyebrow as Aazar settled back into her seat.

"Yeah, it's fine," she replied, her voice neutral. She didn't want Caleb to see the unease that still clung to her. She couldn't afford to show it, not here.

"Good," Caleb said, his voice warm. "We were just discussing how rare it is to find someone like you: someone disciplined and in control."

Johnny snorted lightly. "Disciplined for your type, anyway."

Aazar's gaze snapped to Johnny, her jaw tightening. "What do you mean by my type?"

Johnny leaned forward, his voice low, laced with disdain. "Variants who aren't trained properly. Feral bottom feeders who rely on raw emotion and violence. You know, like The Order."

A chill crept down Aazar's spine, but she forced herself to remain calm, hiding the storm inside. "I'm not a bottom feeder."

Johnny's eyes narrowed, and Aazar could see the suspicion flicker in his gaze. "Don't play dumb, Aazar. Are you telling us you're not affiliated with The Order? Because you sure seem like the type. Aggressive, uncontrolled… dangerous."

Aazar's pulse quickened, but she kept her face neutral. Caleb's voice cut through the rising tension like a knife. "Johnny, that's enough. You're crossing a line."

Johnny ignored Caleb, his eyes still locked onto Aazar's. "Well?"

Aazar met his stare head-on, her voice firm. "I'm not in The Order. I don't have ties to them." It was true enough to slide easily from her lips, but it left a bitter taste.

Johnny didn't look convinced, but Caleb intervened again, his tone more forceful. "Johnny, drop it. You're being rude to our guest."

Johnny scoffed but leaned back in the booth, taking a long sip of his drink. "Fine. But I'm watching you."

Caleb turned back to Aazar, a smooth smile returning to his face. "You'll have to excuse Johnny. He gets paranoid sometimes. We have to be careful, you understand?"

Aazar nodded slowly, keeping her wariness hidden behind a calm mask.

"People want to expose us," Caleb explained, leaning in closer. "Our family's kept our abilities secret for generations. It's why we call ourselves Legacy Variants. The Order brings unnecessary attention, spotlighting Variants and causing panic. Johnny feels strongly about keeping our operations discreet."

Aazar glanced toward Johnny, who was still eyeing her, his suspicion clear. "So, you're Variants, but your eyes: "

"Trained from childhood," Caleb said smoothly. "We control our powers, so our emotions don't alter our eyes. That's why we blend seamlessly."

"Usually, I can tell another Variant by a familiar feeling," Aazar said. "How come I can't feel your Variant energy?"

"We learn how to keep our identities hidden from each other as children, too. There are too many factions that disagree for everyone to know you're a Variant all of the time."

Johnny interjected, still eyeing her with suspicion. "Unlike you and your Order friends, flaunting your abilities like badges of chaos."

"Johnny," Caleb warned again, sharper this time. He shook his head, clearly exasperated. "Look, Aazar, you handled yourself impressively tonight. Your powers, your reactions: it's clear you've seen real combat."

Aazar hesitated and changed the subject. "If you're both Variants, why hire me as security?"

Caleb smiled broadly, a knowing gleam in his eyes. "My powers are effective, but too noticeable. Super speed draws attention. Johnny's power-"

Johnny interrupted, his grin dark and almost predatory. "Let me demonstrate."

Before Aazar could respond, Johnny's voice echoed in her head, clear and chilling: *You should reconsider lying to us.*

Aazar flinched, instinctively pulling back, her heart pounding. Johnny smirked, adding aloud, "Useful, isn't it?"

"And unsettling," she shot back, a cold edge to her voice.

Then she heard her own voice respond back to her as Johnny's smile widened: *You have no idea.*

She blinked, terrified. If he could mimic a person's inner voice, he could manipulate people into doing almost anything. They would think it was their own idea.

Caleb laughed, breaking the tension. "It's invaluable in business, negotiation, and security, but too subtle for direct protection. That's why we need someone like you. Powerful, controlled, and effective."

Johnny eyed her skeptically. "Assuming she's trustworthy."

Aazar's temper flared, but she kept it in check. "I haven't given you a reason not to trust me."

Caleb raised a hand, signaling the end of the conversation. "Enough of this. Let's stop the Variant-on-Variant crime! Let's do shots!"

A woman walked up to the table and took their order. Johnny grimaced as she walked away.

"I don't understand why you always want to be surrounded by Normies, Caleb," Johnny said. "I think they smell weird. It's like they roll around in the mud all day."

"Oh, come on," Caleb said. "Some of them are fun to look at." He glanced at a woman with a short skirt who walked by. "among other things…"

"It's disgusting that you have sex with them," Johnny said.

"Why? They have all the right parts," Caleb snorted.

"They're practically animals." Johnny said.

"Aren't we all animals?" Aazar said.

They both looked at her and laughed.

Caleb leaned over the table. "Don't tell me you worry about Normies, Z. They're barely sentient."

"That's unfair," Aazar said.

"Is it?" Johnny questioned, "They don't feel as deeply as we do. They aren't as strong as us. They can't move or think like us. We're superior in every way. And soon, we'll overtake them as the dominant species."

"Do you really think that?"

Caleb laughed, "Legacies have been saying that for decades."

"It's true," Johnny said. "Our numbers grow daily. In a few years, the Normies will only be good for cooking and cleaning."

"Like slaves?" Aazar said, finding herself more irritated with the conversation than she thought she'd be.

"Let's just change the subject," Caleb said.

Johnny slammed his fist on the table.

"Normies had control of the world for centuries, and we Variants are just now taking control." Johnny started. "We're finally moving in the direction of science, technology, and evolution because we stopped letting the cattle run the farm. We're on the right track."

"Creating a slave race doesn't seem like the right track to me," Aazar said.

Johnny scoffed as Caleb laughed nervously.

The rest of the evening passed in forced pleasantries, the atmosphere strained, but by the time Aazar left the lounge, she was emotionally drained. Johnny's accusations still echoed in her mind, lingering like a shadow she couldn't shake, and the way they talked about the Normies made her uncomfortable. Although Aazar wasn't a fan of Normies for the most part, she didn't think they were less human.

Back home, she found the entire household awake, the tension in the air palpable.

"Aazar!" KJ rushed toward her, his relief evident. "You're okay."

"I'm fine," she reassured him, gently touching his arm. But then her eyes landed on the figure standing quietly in the corner: Flenoid.

The Machine Breathes

The knock on her bedroom door the next morning echoed through the quiet house, making Aazar flinch slightly. She knew it was Flenoid. He'd kept the evening conversation light, but Aazar had rushed to bed in hopes of staving off the true conversation Flenoid wanted to have.

It was early morning, and the sunlight streamed through the windows, casting soft, golden hues across the room. She glanced over at KJ, still peacefully asleep, curled up under the blanket. Aazar sighed as she stood up and padded toward the door.

When she opened it, Flenoid stood in the doorway, his usual stoic expression barely hiding the concern in his eyes.

She wasn't sure what made Flenoid come here from Arizona. They hadn't parted on the best of terms the last time she'd seen him. She hoped whatever he wanted was something easily handled, but she didn't trust her luck.

"You're up early," she remarked, stepping outside the bedroom.

"I didn't want to waste any more time," Flenoid replied, his voice steady as he turned to walk into the Living room. "We need to talk."

Aazar hesitated but pushed the door closed behind her. "Come on," she muttered, following her old mentor into the living room. Simon stirred slightly on the couch but stayed asleep, his form a quiet presence in the room. Flenoid paused to observe him, his eyes scanning the room before returning his focus to Aazar.

"I've heard about who you work for," Flenoid said, his voice low, deliberate.

"And I have a warning for you."

"You can save it," Aazar snapped, "I know who they are. They're rich Variants with a little bit of a God complex, but nothing I can't deal with.

Flenoid shifted his weight uncomfortably before meeting her eyes. "Caleb and Johnny are far more dangerous than that. I know you think you can handle them, but you need to be careful."

Aazar rolled her eyes, "Oh, please."

Flenoid hesitated, his gaze flicking toward Simon before he spoke again, his voice lowered. "I can't tell you everything, Aazar, but Legacy Variants always come across un-intimidating. It's how they're raised, but remember, they're cunning and vicious. I've seen what they're capable of."

The heat in Aazar's chest flared up, frustration rising quickly. She was sick of him being so cryptic. If he'd been more forthcoming when she was with The Order, things might have turned out differently.

"What do you mean, 'you've seen what they're capable of'?" Aazar spat, "You never tell me anything, Flenoid! You always talk in riddles, like everything's a damn secret. Why can't you just tell me what's going on?"

Flenoid stepped back, his face hardening at her outburst. "I can't tell you everything because I'm trying to protect you. The less you know about these people, the better."

Aazar clenched her fists, frustration boiling over. "No. You're treating me like a child who can't make decisions for herself. If you don't tell me why they're so dangerous, I'm not listening to you. This secretive bullshit has to stop."

Flenoid's expression didn't change, but his eyes darkened. "You don't understand the politics of Variants, Aazar. Johnny's family has been in the game for generations. The things they've done: what they're capable of: are beyond what you've seen. You can't just walk into this and think you can handle it on your own."

Aazar's pulse spiked, her voice rising. "You don't think I can handle it?" she spat, the words hot and sharp. "You really think I'm some dumb kid who doesn't know what she's doing? I've fought battles before, Flenoid. I've survived things you wouldn't believe. I don't need you to protect me. I'll figure it out myself."

Simon stirred in his sleep but showed no sign of waking up. Aazar registered his presence and tried to remember to keep her voice down.

Flenoid sighed, his gaze lingering on her. "Just remember what I've said. They act like prey, but they're predators."

Aazar turned away, her fists still clenched at her sides. "Whatever," she muttered. "I've had enough of your warnings." She stormed toward the door, needing space from the conversation, from the tension between them. She hated how he could get under her skin. "I'll take care of it."

Flenoid didn't say another word. He simply turned and left, closing the door quietly behind him.

* * *

The next morning, Aazar arrived at Caleb's office with a quiet determination. She had spent the entire night replaying the events from the previous evening in her mind: the attack, the photo, Avery's handwriting, Flenoid's warning and the sinking feeling that something darker was unfolding. But the more she tried to convince herself to ignore it, the more the unease gnawed at her. The feeling was hard to shake.

The usual polished atmosphere of the office building felt heavier than usual as she entered. The receptionist gave her a polite smile as she passed by, but the warmth of the welcome seemed to dissipate in the air around her. She stepped into the elevator, her reflection staring back at her in the mirrored walls.

The elevator doors slid open, and Aazar stepped out, her shoes thudding against the floor as she walked toward Caleb's office. As she approached, something felt off. The door was slightly ajar, and she could hear voices coming from inside.

Aazar paused, instinctively pausing to listen. One voice was unmistakably Caleb's, but the other two voices were unfamiliar. She recognized the cadence of authority in their tone. Investigators, from the look of them. She took a deep breath, steadying herself, then pushed open the door.

Inside, Johnny stood by the windows, speaking with two men in dark suits, their faces serious and focused. Aazar's heart sank. She could tell immediately that they were detectives when she saw the badges clipped to their belts.

Johnny's eyes flicked toward Aazar as she entered, and a slow smile spread across his face. "Ah, Aazar. Perfect timing."

One of the officers turned to her, his expression unreadable. "We're just getting some details about last night's attack. Trying to find out who was behind it."

Aazar's stomach tightened at the mention of the attack. The last thing she wanted was to get caught up in an investigation, especially not one that could dig into her past. She didn't even know if she wanted to find out who had attacked the limo, but she sure as hell didn't want Caleb and Johnny digging deeper into it. The more they dug, the closer they would come to uncovering things she'd rather stay buried.

"Maybe it's not worth pursuing," Aazar said, her voice calm but firm as she stepped further into the room. "Whoever did it is gone. It was probably a random thief trying to make a quick buck. You'll just be stirring up trouble."

Johnny raised an eyebrow, his smile fading slightly. "You really think so? A Variant was behind the attack, and we don't know why. This isn't something you just forget. We need answers."

The two investigators exchanged a glance, and Aazar felt the tension rising. She tried to remain composed, but she could already sense that this wasn't going to go the way she wanted it to.

"I understand your concern," she said, her voice steady. "But trust me, Johnny, digging deeper won't help. It's better to leave it alone. Focus on the bigger picture. If you keep chasing this, you enemies might take advantage of this distraction."

Johnny's gaze sharpened, and he took a step closer, his eyes narrowing. "You seem awfully keen on stopping this investigation," he said, his voice colder now. "You have something to hide, Aazar?"

The question hit harder than she expected. She took a slow breath, her composure threatened. "I'm just trying to save you the trouble. The last thing you need is to drag something like this out. It's a dead end and a waste of time."

Johnny didn't look convinced. "Or maybe you're just trying to cover your tracks. Maybe you know more than you're letting on."

Aazar could feel the suspicion in his words. She wanted to retort, to demand that he back off, but she knew this wasn't about her. Johnny needed answers. He needed control over a situation he couldn't fully understand. She saw it in the tightness of his jaw, the barely contained frustration in his eyes.

"You've got it all wrong," she said, her voice sharper now. "I'm not trying to cover anything. I'm trying to protect Caleb. Do you really want to make a big deal out of some two-bit hustler?"

Johnny's expression hardened, his gaze flickering between her and the investigators. "I'm not sure I trust you, Aazar," he said, his voice low and dangerous. "Not with something this important. You've been acting strange."

Her chest tightened, but she held his stare.

"How would you know that?" Aazar said. "You don't know anything about it at all."

Johnny's eyes lingered on her for a moment, then he turned back to the investigators. "Keep digging. We'll find out who did this. I want answers."

Aazar felt her stomach churn. She had just become a part of something she didn't want to be involved in. The more Johnny pushed, the closer they would get to uncovering her past. Or worse, Avery's.

As she turned to leave, Johnny's voice called after her. "We'll figure this out, Aazar. You might not like it, but I think you'll want to be around when the truth comes out."

Aazar clenched her jaw, but she said nothing as she walked out of the office. The weight of Johnny's words hung heavy in the air. No matter what she did, the investigation wasn't going away.

Untrained

The low hum of the old computer filled the otherwise quiet room. Aazar sat at the desk, her fingers hovering over the keys. It had been a long time since she'd used a machine like this, and the clunky keyboard felt unfamiliar under her fingertips. She hadn't grown up with electronics; everything she knew about technology had come later in life, after leaving home and after The Order had forced her into a world she hadn't fully understood at the time. But now, here she was, facing a task she never thought she'd have to do: reaching out to Avery.

She sighed, running a hand through her hair, frustrated by her hesitation. She wasn't sure how to word it, but she knew contacting him was the only way to resolve things. The situation had been tense: especially with KJ's growing insecurity whenever Avery's name came up. But this wasn't about that. It was about finding closure, some way to move forward.

Aazar's fingers finally found the keys. She typed carefully, trying to keep her emotions in check.

Subject: Request for a Meeting

Dear Avery,

I hope this message finds you well. It's been a while since we last spoke, and I've had time to reflect on everything that happened between us. I know things ended on difficult terms, but I'd like to ask for the opportunity to meet with you and discuss everything face-to-face.

If you're open to it, please let me know a time and place that works for you.

Thank you,
Aazar

She read over the email again, feeling the weight of the words. It wasn't perfect, but it was simple and honest. Her finger hovered over the "Send" button, her nerves tightening as the silence around her deepened.

"Just do it," she muttered to herself.

She retracted her hand and stood up from the desk.

Suddenly, the door to her room creaked open. She jumped as Logan's head popped around the door frame, a mischievous grin spreading across his face.

"What are you doing?" he asked, leaning against the door, trying to peer at the screen over her shoulder.

Aazar rolled her eyes and turned the screen away from him. "Nothing you need to know."

Logan scoffed, but his curiosity was evident in his eyes. "You're always so secretive, Z. Aren't we like family now? I'm just trying to see what's so important. You never use the computer."

"I said no," Aazar snapped, irritation creeping into her voice. She gestured toward the door as she sat back down. "Now leave. I'm not in the mood."

Logan raised his hands in mock surrender, still grinning. "Fine, fine. But I'm going to find out eventually."

"Find out what eventually?" KJ's voice came from behind Logan.

Aazar exhaled sharply, dread settling in her stomach. She turned toward the computer screen and pressed send quickly before facing KJ.

"What's up?" she asked, trying to sound casual, though the nerves were already creeping into her voice.

Noticing the awkwardness in the air, Logan tiptoed out of the room, quietly shutting the door behind him.

KJ's eyes were locked on her, a frown pulling at his features. "What are you doing on the computer? You usually ask me to handle it if you need it."

Aazar hesitated, caught off guard by his suspicion. Her pulse quickened. "I: uh, I was just sending an email," she said reluctantly, avoiding his eyes.

"For your job?" KJ crossed his arms, his brow furrowing in suspicion.

Aazar bit her lip, the tension between them thickening. She knew he wouldn't take this well, but she couldn't lie to him. She couldn't lie about this.

"To Avery," she finally admitted, her voice barely above a whisper.

KJ's expression changed instantly. His arms dropped to his sides, and his mouth tightened. "What? Aazar, are you serious?"

Aazar closed her eyes for a moment, then met his gaze. "Look, I just wanted to reach out. I thought maybe we could settle things. It's been a while, and I:"

"Settle things? Are you out of your mind?" KJ interrupted, his voice rising with frustration. "You're putting yourself in danger by doing this! You can't just reach out to him like everything's fine! He's been a part of your past for a reason, Aazar. You can't just erase that! He tried to drug you! He just tried to attack you!"

Aazar took a step back, her heart stinging at his words, but she understood his concern.

"I'm not erasing anything," she said quietly. "I just need to stop him from attacking this community, KJ. Johnny is launching an investigation into the limo attack. What if he finds out about our former ties to The Order? We can't just hide forever."

KJ's eyes darkened, frustration and fear etched on his face. "So that's it? You're just going to go right back into the fire? What if he comes after you again, Aazar? What if: "

"I won't let that happen," she cut him off, her voice more forceful than she intended.

KJ's face fell as he paced around the room. "You don't know what you're getting into. I won't sit by and watch you put yourself in harm's way. This whole thing is insane!"

"I'm not asking you to watch, KJ," she said softly, stepping closer to him. "I'm asking you to trust me."

But the moment her words left her mouth, KJ was already heading for the door. "I can't do that right now, Aazar," he muttered, his voice cold. "I need some air."

With that, he walked out, slamming the door behind him. Aazar stood frozen in place for a few seconds, her heart heavy with guilt.

Her housemates, who had been listening from the hallway, started murmuring among themselves, clearly trying to gauge the situation. Aazar didn't care to hear their concerns, but she knew they meant well.

With a sigh, she paced back and forth, her mind a whirlwind of conflicting emotions. She wanted to go after KJ, to make things right, but part of her knew it wasn't the right time. He needed space. And she needed to focus.

* * *

By the time night fell, she was depressed. KJ still wasn't back yet, and she hadn't gotten a response from Avery. What if he didn't respond at all? Or worse, what if he responded by sending another assassin?

She stood up and walked to her bedroom, her footsteps echoing in the empty hall. Sitting on the bed, she reached for her phone and checked her email.

Avery's response was waiting for her.

Subject: Re: Request for a Meeting

Aazar,

I've received your message, and I believe a meeting would be beneficial for both of us. Let's set a time. I'm available in three days, if that works for you.

Best,

Avery

Aazar read it through twice. He agreed to meet. After everything that had happened, after all the years of uncertainty, she finally had the opportunity to understand why he wanted to kill her after all of this time.

Her chest felt both heavy and light at the same time. She was closer to closure, but she knew it wouldn't come easy.

As she lay down to sleep, she couldn't help but wonder how long it would be before she could finally move forward without looking back.

Static

The door slammed shut behind KJ as he slumped into the room, and Aazar turned her head sharply. His movements were unsteady, his eyes bloodshot, and the unmistakable smell of alcohol hung heavily around him. He staggered in the doorway, dragging his feet as though he'd just scaled Mt. Everest. His gaze met hers, and there was something dark in his expression: resentment, anger, frustration: emotions that had been building between them all evening.

"You're back," Aazar said, keeping her voice steady, though her pulse quickened. "Did you have a good time?"

KJ's eyes narrowed, and he took a long, unsteady breath before muttering, "Like that matters to you."

The words hit her like a slap, sharper than she expected. She opened her mouth to respond, but the bite of his words lingered in the air, hanging like an accusation. He threw his jacket on the chair and collapsed onto the couch, rubbing his temples with one hand.

Aazar stood still, her chest tightening. She opened her mouth again, but this time, it wasn't anger that surged up inside her: it was raw honesty, born from a place deeper than either of them wanted to admit.

"Avery accepted my request," she said softly, her voice carrying the weight of the admission. She watched KJ's posture falter, his body stiffening as he froze.

The silence between them stretched thick with unspoken tension.

KJ let out a long, bitter laugh. "Of course he did," he muttered, shaking his head. "Because you always have to go back to him, don't you? You never stop. No matter how much he shows you that he doesn't care about you."

"I'm trying to fix things, KJ," she said quietly, her heart pounding. "I don't expect you to understand, but I have to do this. He put a hit out on me. What if there's one on you, too? We have to see if there's a way to resolve this that doesn't end with one of us dead."

KJ looked up at her, frustration clouding his eyes. "Fine," he spat, his voice harsh, "do whatever you want." He sat on the edge of the bed with his back to her as he took off his shoes.

Aazar's heart twisted, and for a moment, she wanted to say something, anything, to bridge the gap that had opened between them. But the words felt wrong. Instead, she turned away, walking toward the door, needing distance from the weight of the conversation. She knew he was hurting, but she was hurting too. This wasn't just about the past; it was about the future, and she needed to figure it out.

* * *

The next morning, the tension hung heavy in the room like a thick fog. KJ's hangover loomed over the space, his groggy movements and unshaven face adding to the unease between them. They barely spoke. KJ sat in silence, nursing his headache and the anger that had yet to dissipate. Aazar stayed in the kitchen, moving quietly, avoiding unnecessary conversation.

Simon wandered in with a grim expression, and Aazar almost sighed in relief: anything to break the silence.

"Hey, Z," Simon greeted, rubbing his eyes. "Can we talk for a minute?"

Aazar turned from the stove, her curiosity piqued. "Sure, what's up?"

Simon hesitated, glancing at KJ, who was slouched at the table, looking like he was about to pass out. "I've been thinking about this girl at my school," he said, his voice lower, almost uncertain. "She's… different. I think she's a Variant. Do you think you could meet her after work? Help her out like you helped me?"

Aazar's heart softened at the request. She remembered how lost she'd felt when she first discovered her powers: how overwhelming it had been. She was in a position now to help someone else who might be going through the same thing. It didn't matter how much tension there was with KJ, she couldn't ignore the opportunity to support someone else.

"Yeah, I'll meet her," Aazar said with a soft smile. "You're right. I know how hard it was back then, and if I can help her, I will."

Simon's relief was immediate. "Thanks, Z. She's been really quiet about it, so I think she's still trying to figure it out. I just thought… maybe you could talk to her. See if she wants to come to the meetings."

"I'll make time for it," Aazar promised. "After work."

Simon grinned, visibly relieved. "Cool. We'll meet you outside the school, by the buses."

Aazar nodded, her thoughts already shifting to the girl Simon mentioned. She wondered what kind of powers she might have. Was she like Aazar, someone who could control fire? Or was her ability something entirely different?

* * *

Aazar stepped out of the car, her boots striking the cracked pavement with a dull echo. She looked around at the dimly lit street: a narrow alley tucked behind a run-down strip mall, where the smell of bleach and mildew hung heavy in the air. The distant thrum of music reverberated from nearby bars, but this part of town felt quieter, darker, more dangerous.

It wasn't the first time she'd found herself in a grimy neighborhood. Johnny and Caleb always seemed to end up in places like this: gritty, forgotten corners of the city where trouble could pop up at any moment. She didn't know why they liked to hang out here, but she'd learned quickly it wasn't her place to ask. Not directly, anyway.

Her boots clicked sharply against the cracked pavement as she approached the laundromat. A neon sign buzzed weakly above, casting a faint, eerie glow that illuminated the alley. She pushed open the door, the stale air inside hitting her like a wall.

The laundromat had been transformed. Card tables lined the back wall, and a thick haze of smoke hung in the air, adding to the feeling of seclusion. People sat at the tables, eyes darting between their cards and the pile of chips in the center. The smell of stale cigarettes and cheap liquor clung to the walls. The low murmur of voices filled the room, but there was an undercurrent of tension. Every eye flicked toward the door whenever it creaked open, and Aazar could sense that everyone was waiting for something to happen.

Johnny and Caleb were at the table furthest from the door. Aazar moved toward them, leaning against the wall near the entrance, observing the game. She'd been asked to watch their backs, keep an eye out for potential threats, but she wasn't sure what kind of trouble could surface here.

The table was surrounded by three men, their expressions cold and calculating. Their clothes were expensive, but their disheveled appearance told a different story: they were out of place, even in this seedy part of town.

The older man wearing a green reflective vest over a black t-shirt glanced at his cards nervously.

Johnny smiled. "You doing okay there, bud?"

"Worry about yourself," The man snapped. He looked at his cards, and Aazar watched as the confidence drained from his face.

"I fold." He said sadly.

Johnny grinned.

The shuffle of cards and the clink of poker chips filled the room, but Aazar noticed something odd. There was a certain hesitation in the way the players folded their hands. Their eyes flickered nervously between their cards and the pile in the middle, as if something was compelling them to make a decision they weren't fully comfortable with.

"What about you, Earl?" Johnny said, looking casually from his own cards at the short man sitting next to him.

The man swallowed before slamming his cards face down on the table and crossing his arms.

Aazar narrowed her eyes and focused on Johnny. His gaze was fixed on the last player in front of him, unblinking, his face hard and emotionless. But there was something in his stare, a certain intensity that felt almost unnatural.

The man had his chips in his hand, about to call, but suddenly pulled his hand back and sighed loudly.

"I fold."

Then it clicked: Johnny was using his powers.

He was controlling the poker game. Aazar could feel it now, the pulse of his power, faint but undeniable. A quiet tingle in the air that seemed to emanate from him, invisible but potent. His influence was subtle, manipulating the players into second-guessing themselves, pushing them to fold when they otherwise wouldn't have.

It was impressive, unsettling. It was a trick of the mind, and Johnny was too good at it. Too good at making people bend to his will without them even realizing it.

Johnny's gaze flicked toward her, and she quickly looked away, pretending to be casual. But she felt his eyes linger, a smirk creeping across his face.

She heard his voice in her head, clear and chilling: *See something you like?*

Aazar bristled at the smugness in his expression. He knew exactly what she had figured out. She couldn't help but feel a flash of irritation. Johnny had no idea what it was like to have to fight for control over her own mind, to constantly battle against the impulses her powers gave her. To do this to people who had no way to defend themselves was cruel.

She turned her attention back to the table, but the flicker of irritation refused to fade. Johnny's control over his powers was too precise, too dangerous, and it was making her uneasy.

Focusing her thoughts, Aazar gathered a bit of her own power, directing a sharp, pointed swear word toward him in her mind. She wanted to see if he could hear her, if he could catch her thought the same way she had caught his.

She waited, observing Johnny, but there was no response. No flinch, no sign that he'd noticed. Aazar breathed a quiet sigh of relief, realizing that Johnny's powers only worked one way. Todd had been able to read minds, but Johnny couldn't. He was good, but not invincible.

"Everything all right, Z?" Caleb's voice broke through her thoughts. He was grinning, leaning back in his chair, watching her with an amused expression.

Aazar straightened up and shook her head, pushing her thoughts aside. "Yeah, just… watching the game."

"Not a fan of the way Johnny's running it?" Caleb asked, arching an eyebrow.

Aazar hesitated, unsure how to respond. She'd already seen enough to know Johnny was playing a dangerous game, but she wasn't about to call him out on it in front of everyone. Instead, she gave Caleb a tight smile. "Just trying to stay out of trouble."

Caleb chuckled, waving a dismissive hand. "Trouble? This place is a preschool compared to the poker club we went to three years ago." He took a sip of his drink, his eyes flicking back to the table.

Aazar's gaze wandered back to the poker game. The men at the table were clearly uneasy, their hands trembling slightly as they folded. She saw the same reluctance in their eyes, the same forced hesitation.

It wasn't until the man named Earl stood up and left the table in a huff that Aazar realized how badly things had spiraled. Johnny's manipulation had cost this man a hefty sum, but he was too afraid to protest.

"Well, I'm cleaned out," Caleb said, slamming his cards down with a sigh. He looked at Aazar. "Are you ready to leave?"

Johnny glanced away from the table and fixed his gaze on her, that smug grin spreading across his face, clearly enjoying his victory over the other players.

"Sure," Aazar said, her voice tight. "Let's go."

As she turned to leave, Johnny called out one last time, "You've got a good eye, Z. You might want to join the game sometime. Could use someone like you around."

Aazar didn't look back. She didn't need to. Johnny had his power, but she had her own. And she wasn't afraid to use it.

* * *

Later that afternoon, she found herself waiting outside the high school, hands shoved deep into her pockets as the sun cast long shadows across the pavement. Her gaze flicked across the flow of students until it landed on Simon, making his way toward her with a wide grin.

Behind him, a girl Aazar hadn't seen before trailed quietly. She was tall, with long black hair that seemed almost too dark against her pale skin. Her clothes were all black: black jeans, a black over-sized hoodie, and boots that gave her a slightly intimidating edge. The only bit of color on the girl was a light purple streak of dyed hair on the left side of her head. Aazar's first instinct was to categorize her as goth, but she knew better than to judge by appearances alone.

"Hey, Z," Simon greeted, offering a fist bump, which Aazar returned. "This is Monica."

Monica offered a small nod, her lips barely twitching into a smile. She didn't meet Aazar's eyes, her gaze fixed on the ground in front of her.

Aazar smiled warmly, trying to put her at ease. "Nice to meet you, Monica. You hungry? How about we grab some burgers?"

Monica's eyes flicked up to meet Aazar's briefly, a flicker of something: curiosity, perhaps, dancing in her gaze before she looked away again. She hesitated before nodding. "Sure."

Simon was already bouncing with excitement. "Sweet, let's go!" he said, leading the way with his usual boundless energy, making small talk as he rambled about something Aazar only half-listened to. Her attention, however, was on Monica, who walked silently beside them, her posture stiff, as if she were always keeping to herself.

They arrived at a small diner, the kind that served greasy burgers and milkshakes. Aazar led them to a booth in the corner, and they all settled in. Aazar ordered a burger with fries, and Simon immediately picked the messiest item on the menu. Monica remained quiet, her hands folded neatly in her lap, her silence as heavy as it was telling.

"What do you want to eat, Mon?" Simon asked.

The girl almost jumped at the sound of his voice.

"Oh, I don't want anything." She said.

"Come on!" Simon said, "It's Aazar's treat."

Aazar looked at him in surprise.

"What?" He said. "It was your idea!"

Aazar laughed, "Sure, it's on me, order whatever you want."

"Oh, well, I'll just have a salad," Monica said.

As they waited for their food, Aazar noticed how Monica's fingers twitched slightly, as though she was on edge. Aazar's own powers were always there, simmering beneath the surface, but Monica's tension was different. It was quieter, more reserved, yet just as palpable.

Aazar leaned forward slightly, breaking the silence. "So… Monica, what's your power? Simon mentioned you were a Variant."

Monica's gaze flickered to Aazar before looking away again, her lips pressing into a thin line. "I can take memories," she muttered, her voice barely audible.

Aazar sat up straighter, her curiosity piqued. "Take memories? How does that work?"

Monica hesitated, her fingers twitching once more. She glanced around the diner, searching for something, anything, to distract her, before letting out a long breath.

"Here, I'll show you," She said. Monica placed her hands on Aazar's gently. "Think of something you'd never forget. Like your birthday."

"Okay, sure," Aazar said.

Aazar felt a warm sensation go around her head like she'd just put on a hat. The feeling disappeared almost as soon as it came. She didn't feel any different.

"Okay, what's your birthday?"

Aazar opened her mouth to answer, but the date had disappeared from her head. She searched her brain, but she couldn't find the answer. She stared at Monica in surprise.

"It's June 4th," Monica said quietly.

"How did you do that?"

Monica shrugged. "I just touch someone and the memory comes into my head. It's like a USB drive transferring data from one computer to another. The memories disappear from the person's mind and end up in mine."

Aazar leaned back, absorbing the explanation. "So you don't erase them, you just… take them. That sounds intense."

Monica shrugged, nonchalant, but there was an edge to her tone. "Sometimes. But I get paid a decent amount to do it. People come to me with their memories, and I take them away. Stuff they don't want to remember. I take it for them, for a price."

Aazar's frown deepened. "Memories people want to discard can't be good ones."

Monica nodded. "Yeah, but it's not like I have to live through the trauma or anything like that. It's a lot like watching a movie."

Aazar felt a pang of sympathy for Monica, the weight of her words sinking in. It was clear this girl was just trying to survive, but at what cost? "But… is it worth it? I mean, do you ever get used to it?"

Monica shrugged again, the gesture weary. "I smoke a lot of weed. Helps me forget some of the really bad ones and stops the nightmares." She met Aazar's gaze for the first time. "I'm good at compartmentalizing."

Aazar thought about her own power, how she could never truly forget her past. She could control the fire, but she couldn't burn away her memories. "I can help you with that," Aazar said quietly. "With the nightmares. When you can control your power better, you'll probably be able to release memories you don't want."

Monica looked at her in surprise, as if the offer had come from nowhere. "You can help me?"

Aazar nodded. "I can teach you. I've had some experience. I know what it's like to be a Variant and not know how to control it. If you want, I can show you how to keep your power in check."

Monica seemed to consider it for a moment, her expression unreadable. Then, after a long pause, she gave a slight nod. "Alright. I'll try."

Aazar smiled faintly, glad that Monica was willing to try. "Great. You're welcome to come by the house anytime. We can start practicing."

Monica's lips twitched, and Aazar could almost see the faintest hint of a smile forming. "Thanks. I… I appreciate it."

As their conversation shifted to lighter topics, Aazar couldn't help but feel a small sense of accomplishment. She was doing what she had always wanted to do: helping someone who was struggling, someone who didn't have anyone else to turn to. It wasn't much, but it was a start. And for the first time in a long while, Aazar felt like she might be able to make a real difference in someone's life.

Aazar walked home with Simon and Monica, her mind still buzzing from the events of the day. Monica had been quiet the entire walk, which wasn't unusual, but Aazar couldn't help but notice that the girl seemed a little more at ease, almost as if her thoughts were hopeful for the first time in a while. Simon, on the other hand, hadn't stopped talking since they left the diner, making it difficult for Aazar to focus on anything other than his rambling, but Monica didn't seem to mind. She seemed to like hearing Simon prattle on like a child.

When they finally reached the house, Aazar's eyes narrowed in confusion. Several unfamiliar cars were parked in front, and the sound of laughter and music spilled from the living room: voices that didn't match the usual late-night atmosphere of their home.

Simon glanced over at her, grinning. "Surprise!" he said, pulling open the door to reveal a small crowd gathered inside, clinking glasses, chatting, and laughing.

Aazar froze in the doorway, her eyes scanning the room. KJ stood near the center of the crowd, a smile on his face as he chatted with a few of their housemates. The sight of him made her heart skip, but it was the look on his face: unguarded, genuine: that made her take a hesitant step back. Something wasn't right.

"Surprise party?" Aazar muttered, glancing at Simon.

"Yeah," he answered with a teasing smile, "KJ thought it'd be a good idea to bring everyone together to celebrate… well, you."

Aazar raised an eyebrow. "Me?"

"Yup," Simon said, popping the 'p'. "He texted me at school. Something about you having to meet with Avery, and needing support, you know?" He nudged her with his elbow. "Figured we could all pitch in."

Aazar wasn't sure how to feel. She didn't want to be the center of attention, especially after the tension that had built up between her and KJ. But the sincerity in Simon's voice made her soften a little.

She stepped into the room, and immediately, the chatter paused. Eyes turned to her. In the next instant, a cheer broke out, and the group clapped. It was awkward at first, but Aazar gave a shy wave before making her way over to the corner, feeling out of place in the sea of people.

KJ approached her from the side, his grin wide. "I thought we could use a little celebration, especially with everything you've got coming up."

Aazar glanced at him, sensing that there was more to the party than he was letting on. "What exactly is this celebration for?" she asked, a sideways glance accompanying her question.

"It's for you," KJ replied, taking her hand in his. "And for everything ahead. I know it's a lot, but I want you to know we're all behind you."

Before Aazar could respond, the room grew quieter, and KJ took the floor, raising his hands to get everyone's attention. His voice echoed slightly as he began, "Everyone, I've got an announcement. As you all know, Aazar has a big meeting coming up with Avery, the leader of The Order." He paused, letting the weight of the words sink in. "We all know how dangerous things are, but Aazar can't do this alone. She's been handling everything by herself, and we can't let her do that anymore."

Aazar felt heat rise to her cheeks as the room's attention shifted to her. She wasn't sure she was ready to face the group's concerns, especially after everything that had happened between her and KJ.

"I'm going with her," KJ continued, "and the rest of us are going too. We're a team. We stick together, no matter what."

Aazar's pulse quickened. She didn't like him inserting himself like this. They hadn't talked about everyone joining at all. "No," she said firmly, "I'm going alone. I need to handle this by myself. It's not your fight."

Several voices immediately chimed in, and her protests were drowned out by the group's insistent calls. Simon spoke up first, his tone serious. "Aazar, we've got your back. No way we're letting you face Avery and The Order alone."

"I agree," said Logan, walking over from the corner, "this is bigger than just you. We're all in this together."

"I'm with them," Monica added quietly, though she had barely spoken all evening.

Aazar tried to resist, but the truth was, the group's support felt like a comforting blanket, something she hadn't realized she needed. She looked at KJ, who gave her a small, hopeful smile.

She sighed, her shoulders sagging. "Fine. But this doesn't mean I'm happy about it."

The group cheered. KJ stepped forward and took her hands in his, his expression full of apology. "I just want to help, Aazar. I'm sorry for getting drunk and making things harder. I was scared. I'm still scared. But I don't want you to go through this alone. I've learned that I can't protect you by pushing you away."

Aazar softened, squeezing his hands in return. "I should've told you sooner," she admitted, her voice quiet. "I don't want to push you away either."

The tension between them seemed to melt away as KJ's arms wrapped around her in a tight hug.

"I just don't want to put you in more danger," Aazar said softly.

KJ kissed her gently on the forehead, and she decided to drop it for the evening.

After a moment, they pulled away from each other, and the atmosphere in the room lightened. The party resumed, but the mood had shifted. People were chatting again, and Aazar found herself smiling, surrounded by people who were determined to be there for her, no matter what.

As the night wore on, Aazar slipped out into the backyard, needing a moment alone to breathe. The cool air washed over her as she gazed up at the stars. The house was quieter out here; the only sound was the faint rustling of the wind through the trees.

She froze when she saw Flenoid sitting on the grass, his posture relaxed, but his eyes focused on Monica, who was sitting across from him. It seemed like he was talking to her quietly, teaching her something.

Aazar stepped closer, trying not to disturb them. As she approached, Flenoid glanced up, catching her eye. He gave a small nod and gestured for her to sit down beside him.

Aazar lowered herself onto the grass, looking between Flenoid and Monica. "How's it going?" she asked softly.

Flenoid gave a small smile. "I'm helping Monica channel her power. It's not easy, but she's getting there. Your assumption was right. With a little help, she should be able to dispel memories she doesn't want to remember."

Aazar watched them for a moment before speaking. "I owe you an apology. The Legacies are just as dangerous as you said they were. I saw Johnny in action today, and I don't know if I want to be associated with them."

Flenoid's eyes narrowed, but he didn't respond immediately. Instead, he tilted his head, considering her words. "You're beginning to realize it now. Good. But I'm afraid that's only the beginning."

Aazar hesitated before speaking again. "I'm worried, Flenoid. About everything: about Johnny, Caleb, The Order… what I've gotten myself into."

Flenoid leaned back slightly, looking out at the night sky. "You should be worried. But you're also in the best position to find out what they're hiding. Trust them sparingly. I know you're caught up in all of this, but I've seen what happens when people let their guard down."

Aazar frowned, her fingers nervously tracing the grass. "You said Johnny is dangerous, but you haven't told me why. What happened to you? You know more about him than you're telling me."

Flenoid looked at her, his expression softening. "I was once a Legacy Variant."

Aazar's eyebrows raised.

"Really?" She said. "I thought you were an outcast like us after you went…I mean, because of your…your…" She tried to be gentle. "Disability."

Flenoid laughed. "I was born blind, but my ability to sense emotions and energy from other Variants made me a precious commodity. My parents weren't thrilled with a blind child, but I excelled, so they left me alone for the most part."

Aazar waited for him to continue.

"I had everything: wealth, power, influence." He said, "They told me I would never be able to marry, but my life was full."

He turned his back to her. "But when I started teaching poor Variants our techniques, those in charge didn't like it. They didn't want new Variants being able to blend in with them. They wanted to control everything and everyone. I left. I walked away from that world because I didn't agree with them."

Aazar's eyebrows furrowed.

Flenoid looked back at her. "Johnny? Caleb? They've got their own rules. And you're too valuable to be caught in the middle of it all."

Aazar swallowed, feeling the weight of his words. "I won't let them control me."

Flenoid's gaze softened. "That's the spirit. But remember, Aazar, don't let your guard down. Stay alert."

She nodded slowly, taking in his advice. "I will. Thanks, Flenoid."

As they sat in silence for a while, Aazar felt a small sense of peace. It was a fleeting comfort, knowing she had people who cared. But the road ahead was uncertain, and she still had much to prepare for. The calm of the night couldn't erase the storm brewing inside her. She didn't know what was coming next, but she knew one thing for sure: she wasn't going to face it alone.

Violation

The corridor was narrow, all glass and steel, the kind of place that echoes even when no one speaks. Her boots make no sound on the concrete floor. She learned how to do that years ago. Fire doesn't have to announce itself to be dangerous.

Caleb moved first, hands clasped behind his back, posture immaculate. He didn't look over his shoulder to make sure she was still there because he knew she would be. That trust unsettled her more than suspicion ever could.

Johnny lingered to Caleb's right, fingers brushing the wall as if he were reading it. His gaze drifted, unfocused, searching for any unforeseen circumstance.

Aazar kept her expression neutral, but her eyes scanned the area.

"You don't have to look so tense," Johnny said lightly. "If we were in danger, you'd know already."

Aazar didn't respond.

Caleb stopped walking.

The suddenness of it made Johnny halt mid-step, but Aazar didn't break stride. She adjusted, pivoted, and placed herself between them and the open corridor without thinking.

Caleb turns just enough to see her from the corner of his eye.

"Johnny," Caleb said calmly, "leave her alone."

Johnny smiled. It never reached his eyes.

"You're doing well," Caleb said to Aazar. "Exactly as promised."

"I'm not here for praise," Aazar replies.

The silence between the group stretches on as they turn the corner to see a room with a long table in it. Four people are already there. This was clearly the party they were there to meet. Caleb turned to her.

"You'll be accompanying us for this negotiation," he said, "We might need to use Johnny's abilities, and there may be resistance if he's caught."

"I handle resistance," Aazar said.

"And I won't get caught," Johnny said.

"I know." Caleb's gaze sharpens. "I'm just touching base. This is the last component we need to finish the machine, and we need to leave here with it, regardless of how messy things might become."

They resumed walking, and Aazar followed farther behind. For the first time since agreeing to this job, she wondered not whether she could protect them, but whether she should.

Caleb sat down at the table without waiting to be invited, folding his hands on the table as if he owned it. Johnny drifted behind instead, leaning back against the wall, his eyes already roaming their hosts.

Across from them, the three representatives sat in practiced stillness. The woman in the center smiled like she had been trained to do it, and the man beside her kept tapping two fingers against the glass tabletop.

Aazar watched the fingers.

"We appreciate your interest," the woman said, voice even. "But as we explained, our components aren't available for unverified applications."

"Everything worth building starts unverified," Caleb replied pleasantly.

Aazar didn't miss the way the word *building* landed heavier than it should.

Johnny chuckled. "You supply half the city with whatever they want. Are you telling me you draw the line here? Why? To protect Normies?"

"The Normies are irrelevant." The woman said. "We draw the line at this type of technology. We'd be handing a fair amount of power to your House. That kind of monopoly would destroy the balance of our world."

The tapping fingers stopped suddenly as the man looked at Johnny with sudden focus.

"You would profit from this deal too," Caleb said, "Imagine what we could accomplish with the machine. We could stop wars before they start, squash rebellions before they're even thought up. Variants would be clear to solve all of the world's problems. Don't you want your kids growing up in a world like that?"

The woman seemed to think about the offer, but the man with the tapping fingers hadn't moved a muscle in a few minutes.

"It's tempting," She said.

Johnny began to smile subtly. Then Aazar realized it. He was using his power.

Caleb rushed forward, "How about you show us the component and we can work from there."

The woman nodded to the silver-haired man next to her with a brown briefcase in his lap. He placed the case on the table and began to open it, before the man with the tapping fingers placed his hand on the woman's arm. Her eyes hardened.

"It seems that the rules of this meeting have been broken," She said harshly.

"I don't know what you mean…"Caleb began.

"Variant activity has been detected," She said. "Discussion over."

The lights flash red. *Shit*, Aazar thought.

Aazar was shocked when she saw Caleb speed toward the briefcase and snatch it before the man could move.

Glass panels slid down from the ceiling, cutting the room into sections. The doors locked with a solid mechanical sound that echoes in Aazar's chest.

Everything moved at once.

A guard rushed her left.

She pivoted, elbow snapping up, fire flaring instinctively along her arm. The strike landed hard as his skin burned. He screamed.

The smell hit her a second later. Another guard charged toward her. Aazar grabbed him by the collar and slammed him into the wall. The glass blackened under her palm, cracks spidering outward as heat surged before she reined it back in.

Her pulse was loud in her ears. Then Caleb disappeared. The air snapped where he was standing. A chair exploded. Someone hit the floor. Another collapsed before Aazar even tracked the motion. The room couldn't keep up with him. Neither could she.

Super speed. Unfiltered and unforgiving.

"I found an exit!" Caleb shouted, already elsewhere.

Johnny grabbed her arm as another alarm joined the first. "We have to get out of here," he hisses.

She jerked free. "Don't touch me."

The young Variant staggered, clutching his temples, trying to re-calibrate. Caleb reappeared beside him and struck a pressure point in his neck.

The boy crumpled, and they ran toward the back exit.

Aazar barely noticed when she blasted open the door. Aazar threw up shields of heat where she could, burning through barriers that shouldn't burn, keeping the worst of it behind them.

They burst into the open air as they exit the building.

Caleb stopped them a block away in a blink, posture perfect again, breath steady like nothing happened.

Johnny rounded on her immediately. "You attacked the buyer before we could talk to them."

Her hands are shaking. She curls them into fists. "I did my job."

"You made it worse."

"You said you wouldn't get caught." Aazar spat

"That's enough," Caleb said.

Johnny turned away, jaw tight.

"That's it," Aazar said. "I can't do this anymore."

She began to storm down the alley.

"Wait," Caleb said, jogging after her.

"No, Caleb," Aazar said, "This is too dangerous, and I don't even know what I'm doing this for. What kind of machine are you building?"

"You don't need to know that right now," Caleb said. "I'll let you in on it when the time is right."

"No," Aazar said, "I'm leaving."

"Please, stop!" Caleb shouted.

Aazar turned to him.

"I attacked someone," she replies. "I told myself I would never attack someone like that again."

"Listen," Caleb started. "I know things went haywire today, but that was the last component! We won't have missions like that for a while."

"Meaning you no longer need my help."

"There may be another job for you," he continues. "One better suited to your instincts. Less proximity to Johnny."

Johnny bristled, but Caleb didn't look at him.

"Consider it," Caleb said. "Let me make it up to you."

Aazar exhaled slowly. She still needed the money. And if this really was the last dangerous mission, it couldn't hurt to stay on a little longer to find out what they were planning. The fire settled back into her chest, restless but contained.

She nodded once.

"If you're lying, I'm quitting," Aazar said.

"It will be chill," Caleb said, "I promise."

Too Far

Aazar stepped onto the small boat, the salty air of the ocean rushing to greet her, biting at her skin with its sharpness. Caleb's last-minute job offer had come unexpectedly, but he had promised a relaxed, low-key evening, and she had reluctantly agreed. She wasn't quite sure what to expect from the floating house he described as a massive structure of glass and steel. Aazar felt a knot building in her stomach, an unease she couldn't shake.

She had never been much of a water person. Solid ground had always been her refuge, and she didn't particularly like the idea of leaving it behind.

Ten minutes into the boat ride, the motion of the water began to get to her. Her stomach churned, and she clutched the edge of the boat to steady herself. It wasn't just the boat's rocking; the sight of the endless horizon made her feel small, like a single speck in the vastness of the ocean. Her head spun with dizziness, and the rising nausea was becoming hard to ignore.

So this was how it felt to get seasick. Aazar hadn't realized how much of a land lover she was until now. The boat bobbed with each wave, and she tried to keep her focus elsewhere, but the feeling of being off land was unsettling. She found herself wishing for solid ground beneath her feet again.

When the boat finally pulled up to Caleb's floating house, Aazar was grateful for the solid steel deck beneath her. She stepped onto the dock, inhaling the crisp air, trying to shake off the discomfort.

Caleb's place was nothing like she had expected. The enormous structure seemed to pulse with wealth: sleek and modern, built to float. Glass walls looked out over the water, giving the house an almost otherworldly feel, like it had always belonged there, untouched by the worries of the shore. Inside, a poolside party was already in full swing.

Aazar paused, scanning the scene. Laughter and chatter filled the air, blending with the live DJ's music. Chefs were grilling burgers in the corner, and waitresses in skimpy outfits passed by with drinks, the clink of glass punctuating the otherwise relaxed atmosphere.

Her thoughts shifted uncomfortably, remembering the last pool party she'd attended. Peter… Her heart sank. What would Peter think of who she had become? How would he feel about what she'd done to his family?

She shook her head, pushing those thoughts aside. This wasn't the time.

She scanned the crowd again, her eyes narrowing slightly. This was a party, sure, but Caleb didn't really need security here. There was no tension, no sense of danger: just people enjoying themselves, mingling in luxury. She wondered why she'd been invited in the first place. Was this just Caleb's way of distracting her from what really mattered? A subtle attempt to keep her occupied?

Caleb appeared beside her just as she stepped into the party, exuding his usual confidence and charm. He offered her a glass of champagne, his smile warm. Aazar turned it down politely.

"No thanks, I'm good," she said, her eyes scanning the crowd again. She needed this to be over. She had wanted to prepare her group for the meeting with Avery, but now she found herself stuck here. This wasn't what she'd signed up for.

Caleb tilted his head with a playful grin. "Come on, Aazar. Just one glass? I promise, it's the best champagne money can buy."

Aazar shook her head, her mind returning to the things that really mattered. "Caleb, it doesn't look like you really need my kind of security here. Can I head out?"

Caleb's expression softened for a moment, then he leaned in closer, his tone more persuasive. "Stay for a little while. I'll pay you overtime for the extra hours, I swear. I'm trying to pay you back for yesterday. A few drinks, some fresh air. It'll be worth it."

"This isn't really my scene."

Caleb clasped his hands together, almost pleading. The champagne glasses clinked together, and a few drops spilled over the edge. "Please? Johnny can't make it, and I… I want someone here who gets me."

"Why aren't there other Variants at this party?"

"The factions are a little split right now."

"Because of the machine you're building?" Aazar questioned.

Caleb's smile faltered slightly. "What I'm building will change the world. Everyone reacts poorly to change."

Aazar hesitated, glancing back at the lively party. She had other things to do, but Caleb had a way of wearing down her resolve. "Fine," she muttered. "But only for a little while. I'll stay and make sure the house is secure, but I won't be here long."

"Great," Caleb said with a grin. "You'll have a blast, I promise. Why don't you grab a bathing suit from the guest room and join the fun? It'll help you unwind." His hand brushed over her shoulder in a gesture that felt almost fatherly, guiding her toward the house.

The interior of the house was even more impressive than the exterior. Sleek, modern, with walls of glass overlooking the open ocean. Every room was meticulously designed, functional yet breathtaking. Caleb led her through, pointing out his favorite art pieces like a child showing off his drawings. Aazar couldn't help but admire the space, but she quickly snapped herself out of it. This wasn't why she was here.

He stopped at a door and dramatically opened it with a grin. "And this is the guest room. Well, one of them, anyway."

Aazar entered the guest room, taking in the simplicity of the space. The bed was neatly made, and the air smelled faintly of fresh linens and the sea breeze drifting in through the window.

"I'll let you get dressed," Caleb said, stepping out of the room.

As Aazar rummaged through the drawers for a bathing suit, a flash of a memory hit her like a wave.

She froze in place, staring at the bed, her fingers gripping the edge of the dresser. The room reminded her of the first time she had met Norma, the guilt pressing into her chest. The memories she had tried so hard to bury came rushing back. She had been reckless, losing control of her powers, causing harm to people without thinking about the consequences.

Her breath quickened, nausea swirling in her stomach as the weight of those actions came crashing over her. The past was alive in her, suffocating her, reminding her of the darkness she had caused.

"Are you alright?" Caleb's voice broke through her haze of thoughts. He stood in the doorway, a concerned look in his eyes. Had he come in while she was lost in her memories?

Aazar snapped out of it, quickly straightening up. "I'm fine," she said, her voice tight. She could feel the anxiety rising in her chest, but she tried to hold it together.

"I knocked, but you didn't answer." He stepped closer, his presence overwhelming. "You don't look fine."

She swallowed hard, her hand still gripping the dresser. "I just... I just need a minute."

Caleb, though visibly drunk, attempted to show concern. "Hey, it's okay," he said, his voice lower now, comforting. "Take your time. I'm here if you need to talk."

Aazar closed her eyes, biting back the flood of emotions threatening to overwhelm her. She took a shaky breath, then spoke softly, "I'm just: " She hesitated, unsure of how much to reveal. "I lost control once and did things I'm not proud of. And I can't... I can't stop feeling guilty about it."

It was the first time she had admitted it out loud since it happened. KJ had never pushed her to talk about it, but keeping it inside hadn't helped either. Now she was half-opening up to a stranger. This wasn't good.

Caleb's eyes softened, and his tone turned gentler, though his breath still carried the scent of alcohol. "I get it," he said, his voice soothing. "You're not alone, okay?"

Aazar nodded but didn't meet his gaze. His presence felt too close now, the weight of it unsettling her.

Before she knew it, Caleb took a step closer, his hand brushing lightly against her arm. He leaned in, his lips dangerously close to her cheek.

"I'm sorry," Aazar said suddenly, pulling back sharply. The air between them crackled with tension. She couldn't let this happen. "I don't need this right now."

Caleb faltered, his eyes widening. Then his smile twisted, something colder creeping into his features. "What? You're turning ME down?"

"I'm with someone, and I don't see you like that," Aazar rushed, her voice trembling. "Plus, you're my boss."

"Who do you think you are?" he asked, his voice suddenly menacing. "You think you can just walk away from me?"

Aazar recoiled, her heart pounding. "I: " She tried to steady her breath, "I don't want any part of this." Her hands shook now, her pulse racing with the intensity of the confrontation. She could feel the fire building inside her.

Caleb's face twisted with rage, his features contorting into something ugly. He took a step forward, his body radiating fury. "I should fire you where you stand."

The threat hit her like a slap, but she was beyond caring. She turned sharply on her heel and walked quickly out of the room, her hands trembling. She breathed out as she gained control and sprinted toward the dock.

Caleb stood still, his chest heaving with rage, but Aazar didn't look back.

Lost

The ride home felt longer than it should have. The night air seemed colder, the roads darker, and Aazar's thoughts, more tangled than ever. She could still feel the remnants of Caleb's anger lingering in the air, the way his eyes had shifted from concern to rage when she'd rejected him. She had left his house with a storm of emotions swirling inside her, and by the time she stepped through her front door, she was emotionally drained.

As soon as she entered, KJ, who had been watching the news in the living room, caught sight of her. His eyes immediately narrowed, taking in her disheveled appearance: her hair out of place, her face ashen, her movements stiff with anxiety.

"Aazar, what happened?" he asked, his voice thick with concern, his expression clouded with worry. He stood up from the couch and walked toward her.

She didn't answer right away, frozen for a moment in the doorway as the flood of emotions threatened to overwhelm her. She took a few steps forward and dropped her bag onto the floor. Her hands trembled, her mind still reeling from her conversation with Caleb, from the revelations about Johnny and the Legacy Variants, and the confusion and fear that churned inside her.

KJ noticed her hesitation. His brows furrowed as he gently touched her shoulder. "Aazar, talk to me. What's wrong?"

Aazar took a deep breath and walked past KJ to the couch, sinking into it heavily. She was too exhausted to hide it anymore. If there was ever a time to be honest, it was now. She looked up at KJ, who was still standing, waiting for her to speak.

She met his gaze, her voice quiet but steady. "Caleb and Johnny… they're Variants, but they're different." She paused, her throat tight with the weight of the truth. "They're powerful. They come from a long line of people: Legacy Variants, they call themselves. And… I don't know what they're planning, but it can't be good. I think they are going to hurt people. And Caleb tried to kiss me tonight…"

KJ's face shifted instantly, his eyes narrowing, a flicker of something dangerous passing through them. "Wait… what? Caleb tried to kiss you?" His voice was low, his anger barely contained.

She nodded, her stomach twisting. "It was awful."

"I'll deal with him," KJ said, his jaw tightening.

Aazar shook her head, her heart aching. "KJ, don't worry about it. I handled it."

KJ paused, his mind clearly processing the information. His gaze met hers, frustration flickering across his features. "How long have you known they were Super Variants?"

"Legacy Variants," Aazar corrected softly.

"Whatever," KJ bristled, his voice rising slightly.

"Only a couple of days."

His eyes widened. "Why didn't you tell me sooner?"

Tears stung the back of her eyes, and she struggled to hold them back. "I didn't want to get you involved."

But KJ didn't seem to hear her. His fists clenched at his sides as he paced a few steps away, clearly struggling with something inside. "Aazar," he said, his voice breaking, "You should've told me. You should've trusted me. I thought we were past all this secrecy. Why would you keep something like this from me?"

"I didn't mean to hide it from you," she whispered, her voice cracking. "I just didn't know how to handle it. I didn't know if you could handle it. You don't understand, KJ. Legacy Variants are dangerous. They're ruthless."

KJ's jaw tightened, frustration flaring in his eyes. "Aazar, you're making this harder than it needs to be. You're always keeping things from me. Secrets, lies. You're shutting me out again, just like you always do. And I can't take it anymore."

Aazar stood up quickly, stepping toward him, her heart pounding. "KJ, please, don't: "

"No, Aazar," KJ cut her off, his voice rising. "I'm done. I've been through this too many times. Every time things start to get serious between us, you keep secrets. You think you can protect me by keeping everything to yourself, but it's not working. It never works." He exhaled sharply, turning away from her and running a hand through his hair. "I can't do this anymore. I don't want to be in a relationship where I'm always kept in the dark, always wondering what you're hiding from me. I can't keep doing this."

Aazar's breath caught in her throat. "No, KJ, please. Don't say that. I never meant to hurt you. I: "

"You're not listening to me!" KJ shouted, his voice full of hurt and anger. "I'm trying, Aazar. I'm really trying to be there for you, but you don't trust me. You keep pushing me away, getting into trouble, and I can't deal with it anymore. It's too much, okay? I can't deal with it anymore."

Aazar's chest constricted as his words hit her like a wrecking ball. "So, you want to end this? Just like that?"

KJ's face contorted with frustration and pain. He shook his head, as if struggling to find the right words. "I'm not saying I want to end everything with you, but I can't be in a romantic relationship where I don't feel like I'm trusted. I can't do it. But…" He looked at her, his eyes softening slightly. "I'll still go to the meet-up with Avery. I'll still protect you. But I'm not going to pretend everything's fine between us when it's not."

The words hit her like a physical blow. "So that's it?" she asked quietly, the weight of his decision sinking in.

KJ nodded, his shoulders sagging. "Yeah. I need some space, Aazar."

He walked to the bedroom, his footsteps heavy with finality. Aazar stood there, feeling as though the ground had been ripped out from under her. Her chest ached, and the sting of his words lingered. She could feel the tears threatening to spill, but she fought them back. She didn't want him to see her like this. When he returned, he had his pillow in his hand.

"KJ…" she whispered, but he was already heading toward the couch.

Without another word, he laid down, his back to her. "I'm staying on the couch. Don't worry about me."

Aazar stood frozen for a moment, her hands trembling at her sides. She opened her mouth to speak, but the words wouldn't come. Slowly, she sank into the chair nearby, her body heavy with exhaustion.

The sound of KJ's breathing across the room was deafening. It was the only sound in the room, and it made Aazar's chest tighten further.

She closed her eyes, trying to gather herself, but everything felt so broken. The guilt from hiding things from KJ, the fear of what Caleb and Johnny might want, and now the sharp pain of knowing she had pushed KJ too far. It was all too much. She had made so many mistakes, and now she had no idea how to fix them.

She stood and rushed into the bedroom, shutting the door behind her. She collapsed onto the bed alone, her hands pressing to her face as the tears finally fell. She cried quietly in the darkness.

Hours passed, and Aazar found herself staring at the ceiling, her body rigid with silent sobs. The world felt impossibly heavy, and she knew that things between her and KJ might never be the same.

As the night wore on, she wiped her face, trying to gather the strength to sleep. But sleep never came. The silence between her and KJ seemed louder than anything else, and she couldn't escape the constant ache in her chest.

She got up from the bed, unable to stay still, and stood by the window, gazing at the night sky, wondering how everything had come to this. She could feel the weight of her choices, and she knew the road ahead would only get more complicated.

Finally, she let out a long, shaky breath and opened the bedroom door as quietly as possible. She peeked out, seeing KJ's figure on the couch, barely visible, but his shallow breathing filling the room. She couldn't understand how he could be sleeping. She still wasn't sure how to fix things with him, but she knew one thing for certain. The guilt and pain from this moment would stay with her until she figured it out.

And she wasn't sure how long that would take.

Up in Smoke

The desert air was thin and sharp as the wind carried specks of sand across the cracked plateau. Aazar stepped out of the van first, her boots crunching against the gritty terrain. Behind her, KJ, Monica, Simon, and a few of the newer recruits exited. The air between them was tense: not from fear but from anticipation. This meeting with Avery had been a long time coming, and none of them knew what to expect.

"You sure about going in alone?" KJ's voice, soft and tired, broke the silence.

Aazar nodded, her face unreadable. "I have to. It was the condition."

KJ looked away, jaw clenched. "Just remember we're here if you need us."

She gave him a small nod before stepping forward. KJ had been cordial, but the rift between them was undeniable, the tension thick in the air. She pushed it down as best as she could, focusing instead on the meeting ahead. Avery would be looking for weaknesses, and she refused to give him one.

The terrain sloped down into a wide arroyo, where an old cement structure lay half-buried in the earth. It was once a water treatment facility, abandoned when the droughts made it obsolete. Now, it served as a neutral zone for The Order and Aazar.

The door creaked open as she stepped inside. It took a moment for her eyes to adjust to the dim light. Avery was already there, seated on a concrete block like he owned the place. His appearance hadn't changed much: same sharp jawline, same calculating, eerie green eyes, but now they watched her with wariness, not tenderness.

"So you showed," he said flatly. "Guess that counts for something. Especially since the last time we met, you threw a fireball at my head."

Aazar crossed her arms, meeting his gaze head-on. "You deserved it."

He chuckled, but it was hollow, the smile never quite reaching his eyes. "You always did have a flair for dramatics."

Avery stepped forward, eyes scanning her. "You cut your hair." He reached out, as though he wanted to touch it, but she instinctively took a step back, the flicker of heat inside her almost escaping.

Avery noticed the movement and pulled his hand back, slipping it into his pocket.

Aazar cleared her throat. "We need to talk about the Legacy Variants."

Avery's eyebrow rose. "Interesting that you'd bring them up first. Are you worried about your new 'friends'?"

"They aren't my friends."

"Are you sure?" Avery asked, a glint of something sharp in his eyes. "Because you seem pretty chummy to me."

Aazar tried to steer the conversation. "Is that why you put a hit out on me?"

"You're too powerful to be working with my enemies. I had to put a stop to it." Avery said.

Aazar sighed, exasperated. "I think you should focus on attacking them, instead of harassing me."

Avery almost laughed. "Wait…did you think that attack was about our past relationship?"

"Wasn't it?"

Avery stood, his gaze turning steely. "Those Variants you've been hanging around with? They're not just rich kids with powers. They're architects of systems. They own cities, governments, networks. We're pawns to them. All of us."

"So you try to have me killed?" Aazar said, "Why didn't you reach out and try to talk?"

"We aren't school children, Aazar," Avery said. "It's war."

"I just can't believe you were that afraid of me," Aazar said. "You know me."

Avery regarded her for a moment before continuing. "You are…formidable. And I wasn't sure how you would react to meeting me again."

They stood in silence for a second.

Avery brightened. "Since you are open to talking, I would much rather have you back on my side…"

"…Which is why you agreed to this meeting," Aazar finished, her voice a little sharper now.

Avery gave a small smile. "You've always known me better than anyone else."

Aazar ignored the comment. "So what? You think we can take them down together?"

Avery was quiet for a moment, his eyes scanning her face as though weighing her. "Maybe. But I also know you. You don't trust anyone. Especially not me."

Aazar clenched her fists at her sides, the frustration bubbling up. "You're right. I don't. The last time I did, you lied to me and tried to drug me."

"I tried to protect you."

"You manipulated me," she snapped. "There's a difference."

"What was I supposed to do?" Avery spat. "You had lost your mind! Have you forgotten about the five-alarm fire you started in my camp? The prisoners you murdered?"

Aazar's face flushed, but she didn't speak. The words stung, but she had nothing to say.

Avery smiled coldly. "How is KJ by the way? Todd would like a word. He wants to know how you convinced his brother to become a traitor."

Her temper flared, and a burst of heat radiated from her. "Don't bring KJ into this."

"Why not?" Avery snapped, his voice growing sharp. "You brought him into everything else. You dragged him into your war, your guilt, your trauma. And now you're hesitating because you know he's given you everything, but it's still not enough."

Flames flared at Aazar's fingertips before she could stop them. Her body trembled, but she fought to contain the fire. She hated how easily he got under her skin. She felt like a child when he was around. "Shut up, Avery. You don't know me anymore."

He tilted his head, his eyes narrowing. "Don't I?"

Aazar raised her hand to attack, but with a flick of his wrist, he slammed her into the wall, knocking the breath from her lungs. She hit the ground hard, but sprang into a crouch, fire erupting in her palms.

The battle had begun.

From outside, KJ and the others saw the burst of fire through the cracked glass of the old facility. Without hesitation, they surged forward.

Aazar hurled a stream of fire toward Avery, but he countered with a gust of wind that twisted her flames into a cyclone and tossed them harmlessly aside. Her eyes widened. He was using telepathy to manipulate the air directly. Avery must have learned it just to fight her.

Logan charged forward but was slammed into the wall. A deafening crack rang out as his body crumpled to the ground.

"Aazar!" KJ shouted, but his voice was drowned out by the chaos.

Aazar advanced again, blasting heat at the floor to distract Avery as she lunged forward.

He was ready.

Her ankle was snatched from under her, and she slammed onto her back, winded. KJ burst into the room, throwing a bolt of lightning at Avery, who dodged it with ease.

"You okay?" KJ called.

"Yeah. Go!" Aazar urged.

Simon sprinted inside next, flinging glowing shards of light toward Avery. Avery ducked and summoned a wave of pressure that sent Simon skidding back. KJ followed, sending a deep pulse of kinetic energy into Avery, knocking him off his feet.

But Avery wasn't done. He twisted mid-fall, launching a blade of compressed air toward KJ. Aazar quickly threw up a firewall, her powers surging now that her friends had her back.

"You brought the whole damn camp?" Avery shouted, mockery dripping from his voice.

"You left me no choice!" Aazar shouted back.

Together, they surged forward. KJ created shock waves, Simon provided cover fire, and Monica took Avery's recent memories, confusing him. For a moment, it worked. Avery staggered, eyes darting as timelines bent around him.

Aazar channeled every ounce of rage and power into one final fireball, hurling it toward him with a scream.

The impact cracked the wall behind Avery, flames engulfing the air.

When the smoke cleared, Avery was gone.

Burn marks scorched the ground, but there was no trace of his body. Only his voice remained, echoing through the crumbling facility.

"The offer stands, Aazar. Think it over."

She stood in the silence, heart pounding, the flames in her hands finally dying down. Her friends surrounded her, breathless but alive.

They had won. But it didn't feel like victory.

It felt like the beginning of something worse.

Empty

azar stood at the edge of the fire pit in the backyard, the flames flickering in the gentle wind, casting orange shadows across her face. The others were inside, tending to Logan, whispering about their next move, licking their wounds. But Aazar couldn't bring herself to join them. Not while her hands still trembled. Not while the burn of everything she couldn't say still simmered in her chest.

KJ hadn't looked at her. Not once. Not since the battle ended.

He'd checked on Logan. Spoken to Flenoid. Given Simon orders. But her? Nothing. Not even a glance.

She thought back to the fight: Logan's body crashing to the ground, her flames lighting up the twilight, Avery's voice echoing in her head. And KJ: fighting beside her, still choosing to protect her even when he couldn't stand her. That part hurt the most: that he loved her enough to keep her safe, but not enough to stay close.

Aazar stared into the fire and clenched her fists. She had no right to want more. Not after everything she'd done. KJ had trusted her with his whole heart, and she handed him pieces of it only when it was convenient, only when she couldn't avoid it any longer.

But she hadn't meant to become this version of herself. After the Belize's death, she became the one who held everything in until it shattered her. The one who cried alone in supply closets, who erupted in rage before calming down in corners. The one who loved fiercely and still somehow pushed people away.

She had always been that girl, even before the fire. Even before her eyes changed and her life spun out of control.

Aazar pressed a hand to her heart. She couldn't feel her pulse: only the ache.

She bit the inside of her cheek and turned her eyes to the stars, wishing she could unmake the past few years. Wishing she could go back to the start. Back before The Order. Back before Peter died. Back before power made her feel both invincible and unbearably alone.

The sliding door creaked open behind her.

She didn't turn around.

Flenoid's footsteps were soft on the grass as he settled beside her, crossing his legs like they had all the time in the world.

"Logan's stable," he said quietly. "He'll limp. Maybe always. But he'll live."

Aazar nodded, the weight of his words pressing into her chest.

"You okay?" Flenoid's voice was gentle, like he knew the answer but was giving her space to speak.

She hated that question. Hated it because it was too small for what she felt. Hated it because it never had an answer that fit.

"I'm alive," she said, her voice flat. "That's all I've got right now."

Flenoid was silent for a while. He didn't push. Didn't press.

And for that, Aazar was grateful.

"I know things between you and KJ are hard," he said softly, "but pain doesn't always mean it's over. Sometimes it means something's still alive."

She shook her head, a bitter laugh escaping her. "I don't think I know how to fix anything anymore."

"You're not broken," Flenoid said, his words simple but heavy with meaning. "Just bruised. Deep down. The kind of bruising that takes time."

Aazar didn't answer.

"I suppose it's time you knew more about the Legacy Variants since Avery has revealed he plans to fight them," Flenoid continued, his voice lowering, as if sharing something forbidden.

Aazar clenched her jaw. "Why does Avery want to fight them?"

"Because if he wins," Flenoid said, leaning in closer, "he becomes what they are. The leader. The new bloodline. Avery doesn't just want freedom. He wants a legacy of his own."

The air around them seemed to freeze. Aazar didn't speak for a long time.

"He thinks you're on their side," Flenoid added quietly.

Aazar nodded, the weight of his words settling heavily on her shoulders. "And he clearly has spies everywhere. He knew every move I've made in the last few weeks."

Flenoid sighed. "He also sees the conflict in you. That scares him."

"What scares you?" Aazar asked, her voice quieter now, curious.

Flenoid's gaze met hers, his eyes clouded, weighted with something Aazar couldn't quite read. "That you'll become one of them. Not by blood, but by heart. That you'll start believing you're above the people you protect."

Aazar rolled her eyes, her mind flashing to Caleb's attempt to kiss her. "I could never be like them."

Flenoid didn't respond right away, his gaze drifting far off into the night. He seemed lost in thought. "You think I'm already on that path?" Aazar pressed.

"No," he replied, his voice steady. "But paths are made by walking. And you're standing at a fork."

Aazar's posture stiffened. Flenoid looked up at the stars, as though drawing the words from the sky. "Legacy Variants didn't just inherit their power. They engineered it. Twisted their bloodlines over centuries to preserve the strongest gifts. Pyrokinetics married telepaths. Seers married healers. It wasn't love. It was business."

Aazar's frown deepened. "So… it's eugenics."

"Exactly," he said, tapping the rim of his mug. "They call themselves noble Houses now. You've met two. Caleb's from House Corvinus. They specialize in speed and charm. Johnny comes from House Virelli. Telepaths. Spies. Mind-meddlers."

Aazar flinched. "And they control California?"

"The Islands, yes. But their influence stretches farther than you think. Arizona. Nevada. Parts of New Mexico. Some cities haven't passed a single bill without a Legacy whispering behind the curtain."

"They're building some kind of machine that's supposed to change the world, but I don't know what it is or what it does. Do you think it has something to do with how they plan on taking over the world?"

"I don't know, but Legacies have never had world peace in mind when they create things."

Aazar looked away, the enormity of it all sinking in. Aazar didn't answer. She didn't need to.

Flenoid stood and placed a steady hand on her shoulder. "If you face the Legacies, do it with your eyes open. Not every battle is fought with fire."

Yellow Hibiscus

The flowers arrived just before dawn.

Aazar had been awake for hours already, curled up on the couch, a blanket draped over her legs, watching the shadows stretch and shift across the floor. The bouquet was obnoxious: bright, tropical blooms that didn't belong anywhere near the house. Gaudy orange and pink lilies, enormous yellow hibiscus, and a handful of orchids that still smelled like the sea. She didn't need to look at the card to know who had sent them.

Caleb. He'd been calling since yesterday, but she'd been ignoring him.

She let the flowers sit on the entry table, unopened. KJ passed by without a glance. He had stopped looking at her, at anything to do with her, days ago.

The call came around noon. She didn't answer the first time. Or the second. But the third ring, just as she stood in the kitchen debating whether she had the energy to eat, made her answer.

"Aazar," Caleb's voice crackled through the line, tight with something she couldn't place. Shame, maybe?

She didn't speak.

"I just wanted to make sure the flowers arrived," he continued quickly, as though his words were a shield. "I know they're not enough. Nothing would be. I was drunk and… out of line. What I did, what I said, none of it was okay. You didn't deserve that. Especially with how upset you were."

Her jaw tightened. She still hadn't forgiven herself for freezing up in that guest room. Her body had remembered before her mind did, and the memory of Norma's screams had locked her in place.

"You threatened me," she said flatly.

"I know. I know I did," Caleb replied, softer now. "I panicked. I lashed out. But I swear to you, Aazar, it wasn't about power or... entitlement. I was just a drunk idiot who didn't know how to handle being vulnerable around someone like you."

"Why are you calling?" she asked, the annoyance bubbling up. "Because you're sorry, or because you still want me to come back?"

He hesitated. Then, as always, Caleb leaned into charm like it was armor. "Both."

Aazar leaned against the counter, staring at the wilted hibiscus. "I'll think about it."

"That's all I'm asking," Caleb said quickly. "Just think about it. I need someone like you on my team, Aazar. Especially now. And... I miss having someone who actually tells me the truth."

She hung up before she could say anything else.

The truth was, she might need him. Or at least access to his world. If the Legacy Variants were as powerful and corrupt as Flenoid said, then staying close to one might be her only way of figuring out what they were planning. She couldn't afford to be blind to that. Even if it meant working beside the same man who made her skin crawl.

She walked to the front door, picked up the bouquet, and tossed it into the trash.

Maybe she would think about it. But she didn't have to like it.

The door creaked open behind her.

"You're gonna want to hear this," Flenoid said, his voice calm, cutting through the quiet.

Aazar followed him into the living room, where a dusty map had been spread across the coffee table. The group stood around it, eyes nervous, faces tense. Circles marked various cities, most clustered along the West Coast.

"Legacy strongholds," Flenoid said, his finger tracing the red and blue markings on the map. "The red ones are confirmed. The blue? Suspected."

Aazar's gaze locked on the biggest red circle: Los Angeles.

"They hold L.A., San Diego, Santa Cruz... and the northern tip of the

California Islands," Flenoid continued. "Some say the Legacies engineered the secession movement in the first place. An experiment in self-rule. Their rule."

Aazar let the words settle in her mind.

"And Avery wants to take them down here," he added, tapping the map near the Islands. "In the heart of their territory."

Flenoid nodded. "He sees opportunity. Chaos. Room to move. But he doesn't want to dismantle them. He wants to take their throne."

Aazar blinked, the weight of his words pressing in. "You're sure?"

Flenoid didn't answer. He didn't have to.

"Can we fight back against either of these groups alone?" Aazar asked, her voice low.

"Not a chance," Flenoid said. "We're going to have to pick a side."

Her stomach turned. The old Avery had always talked about building something better. But this version of Avery, the one with armies, spies, and a hunger for power, felt like a stranger. And worse, he thought she was working against him.

After the long, bitter meeting that started as a strategy session, the group had unraveled into finger-pointing and splintered loyalties. Half of the group wanted to join The Order, and the other half wanted to stay out of it.

Simon had been the loudest.

"We can't let these Legacies continue!" he'd shouted, half on his feet. "If we have to join with The Order, so be it. This is war. Sure, we had a rough start with an alliance, but we need them."

Monica had backed him up, her dry, apathetic tone cutting through the tension. "We either join The Order or get picked off one by one."

But Hugo...

"You think starting a war with the Legacies is a good idea?" he'd said, his voice quieter than the others, but every word biting. "You think war makes us safe? This isn't leadership. This is an obsession. This is ego. The Legacies have had control this whole time and never bothered us. We should just leave it alone."

That had shut the room up. It was the first time Aazar had felt genuinely small since the fight.

* * *

The hallway outside Logan's room was dark, except for the thin moonlight beam slicing through the cracked blinds. Aazar stood for a moment, her hand hovering near the doorknob. Her heart beat low and slow, like a warning drum echoing from deep inside her chest.

She knocked once, barely audible. Logan's voice came through, tired but awake. "Yeah."

She opened the door. The small bedside lamp cast a faint golden hue over the room. Logan sat propped up against his pillows, a book face down on his lap. His leg was heavily wrapped from the knee to the ankle. His crutches leaned against the wall, silent witnesses to the night's chaos.

Aazar stepped in and quietly shut the door behind her.

"Hey," she said softly.

"Hey," Logan echoed, his voice even, unreadable.

She crossed the room and sat at the edge of his bed, careful to keep a respectful distance.

"How's the leg?"

"Hurts," he said. "But you know. I'll live."

Aazar looked down at her hands, fingers twitching with unspent energy. There was so much she wanted to say. So many apologies. So much guilt.

"Logan, I… I should've pulled back sooner. I saw what was happening and I still-"

"Don't," he interrupted gently. "Don't do that thing where you try to carry it all."

She looked at him, startled.

"You didn't do this to me," he said, his voice calm. "Avery did. Or whatever plan he set in motion. You fought. We all did. That's the risk we signed up for."

Aazar nodded slowly, lips pressed into a thin line.

"But you're hurt," she said, her voice quieter now. "You'll have that limp forever. And I keep wondering if this was worth it. If what I'm doing is really saving anyone."

Logan's gaze drifted to the ceiling, his expression unreadable. "Maybe you should ask a different question. Not if it's worth it… but who you're willing to be for the fight."

The silence stretched, heavy and fragile.

He turned to her again. "I know you're trying. But this thing you've taken on… It's going to change you. Maybe it already has."

That landed like a blow. Aazar stared at him, her throat tight.

"I'm still me."

"Then do you what you need to do to keep being you," Logan said softly.

She left the room not long after, walking back through the hall in silence. Her fingers brushed the wall once for balance. Everything felt thinner, quieter, like the house itself was waiting.

In the main room, Simon and Monica sat on the couch, their expressions tense. A low argument had been rumbling earlier, but it stopped when Aazar walked in. Monica stood, eyes hard but loyal. Simon's jaw was tight, but he gave her a small nod.

"You okay?" Monica asked.

"No," Aazar said. "But I know what I have to do."

C.E.I

The boat rocked slightly beneath Aazar's boots as she stepped onto the polished deck of the floating Legacy Rehabilitation Center for the Homeless. The salty air stung her skin, and she had to clench her jaw, swallowing hard to keep the nausea at bay.

Aazar had decided to work with the Legacy Variants for a few more weeks. She needed the funds to equip her team for the coming war with The Order and to bolster their numbers. Avery couldn't be trusted: she knew that much. Caleb and Johnny weren't much better, but Avery's resentment toward her could sabotage whatever fragile alliance they could still form. The Legacy Variants had been in charge for decades and hadn't destroyed the world yet. The Order, however, was a far more unpredictable threat.

Caleb was waiting at the top of the steps when she reached the platform, sunglasses perched on his head, hands in his pockets. The salty air tousled his styled hair, but he still looked like he belonged on the cover of a coastal billionaire magazine.

"Aazar," Caleb said, his voice a touch softer than usual. "Before we go in, I want to say something."

She arched an eyebrow. "Alright."

"I'm sorry about the party," he began, his voice low, almost drowned out by the wind. "I crossed a line. I was drunk, but that's no excuse. Threatening your job… trying to kiss you… it was wrong. You didn't deserve that."

Aazar's eyes narrowed as she studied him. There was no power play in his posture today, no smug grin. Just discomfort, and a hint of shame.

"Thank you," she said finally, but her tone was sharp. "But don't ever do that again. You pull something like that, and I don't care how powerful your family is. I walk."

He nodded once, his expression serious. "Fair."

She didn't linger. "Let's get on with it."

Inside, the facility gleamed: sterile white walls, chrome handrails, the sharp scent of antiseptic. Caleb gave her a quick tour, explaining that the floating center was "a place for healing," a wellness-focused rehabilitation hub for those recovering from trauma or variant-related events.

Aazar half-listened, but her mind was preoccupied, scanning the space for exits and potential threats. Caleb greeted doctors and engineers like old friends, laughing loudly and making sure every camera caught his best angles.

They passed through various rooms where patients lounged, some hooked to IVs, others meditating. It wasn't until an hour had passed, with the sun fully risen, that Aazar excused herself to find the restroom. Caleb waved her off with a grin, too deep in conversation with one of the architects to notice her hesitance.

She walked briskly down the hallway, turned a corner, and stopped.

The air shifted before the light did. The hallway dimmed, and the scent changed: sanitized metal giving way to something older, sourer. She passed a door that was cracked open and paused. Her breath caught in her throat.

There was a hum: low, electric, and underneath it, breathing. Not one voice, but many. Shallow. Strained.

She pushed the door open farther.

Rows of humans lay in chairs that reclined too far back to be comfortable. Each was strapped in, heads bound in sleek, tight-fitting helmets that covered their ears and wrapped around the base of their skulls. Thin wires fed into their spines, their temples. A few trembled. Others wept silently. All were unconscious.

The machine at the center of the room pulsed with light, delicate tendrils reaching into ports and neural interfaces. Screens flickered with images: memories, she realized. Children. Lovers. Birthdays. Fear. Pain. Regret.

Each one flickered across the screen before blinking into nothingness. Erased.

Aazar's hand flew to her mouth.

"Beautiful, isn't it?"

She spun around, flames flickering behind her eyes, before she saw him. Caleb stood in the doorway with his usual relaxed posture, hands in his pockets like they were back at a pool party.

"What the hell is this?" she hissed, barely managing to contain her voice.

"Our future," he said, stepping beside her and gesturing toward the machine like a proud parent. "The Legacy Council's greatest achievement. We call it the Cognitive Extraction Interface."

"Those are people," she snapped, her voice rising. "Humans."

"Well, sure, but they're just Normies," Caleb said, unfazed. "And they're contributing more now than they ever could have in the world we gave them."

She took a step back. "You're killing them."

Caleb sighed, as if she were being difficult on purpose. "The process is invasive, yes. And sometimes fatal. But the information they give us? It's priceless. Fear patterns, emotional maps, even subconscious cues. We can prevent rebellion before it begins. We can stop a war before it becomes a threat. We can maintain order."

"By erasing who they are?" Aazar's voice shook.

"By learning from them and downloading their consciousness," he replied. "What they are. What they need. And how to keep them from hurting themselves, or us."

Aazar's fists clenched at her sides. Her body shook with restrained power. She couldn't breathe. The flames inside her screamed for release.

"They're not animals, Caleb."

"They're not us," he said calmly. "And you know that. We both do. Someone has to control the Normies. They get out of control when left to their own devices. Surely you see that by now."

Aazar stared at him, really looked at him. His face was clean, well-rested, and pampered. His eyes held no guilt. Only confidence. Belief.

She lowered her head, swallowing hard. Now wasn't the time to show her disagreement.

"You're right," she said softly. "I overreacted."

Caleb smiled, visibly relieved. "I knew you'd see reason. I really do value your insight, Aazar. You're one of the few who get it. Who can handle what's necessary."

Aazar nodded, though her stomach churned. "Can we go back now?"

He offered his arm. She took it, but the weight in her chest remained.

As they made their way back through the hall, Aazar's mind raced. She would reach out to Avery tonight. Taking down this facility was the most important thing to do right now. She needed help.

The Legacy Variants had drawn a line in the sand, and now she knew what lay behind it.

If Avery wanted to burn this place down, maybe, for once, he had the right idea.

Old Habits

The wind off the coast had a dry bite, the kind that clung to Aazar's skin long after the sun dipped low. She adjusted the hood over her head, walking with deliberate steps, her eyes forward, her gait calm. No one questioned her when she said she was headed into the city for a supply run. She'd done it enough times that it had become routine: predictable. Invisible.

That was the goal.

She arrived at the crumbling ruins of an old textile plant just after twilight. The windows were shattered, and the walls were more graffiti than brick. It was a place where people disappeared. The perfect place for a meeting.

Avery stood in the shadows near what had once been a vending machine, his blue eyes muted beneath tinted lenses. He didn't move when she approached.

"You came alone," he said, voice flat.

"You asked me to."

"And you actually listened. Growth."

Avery had become more sarcastic, more blunt since they'd been apart, and she didn't like it.

She narrowed her eyes. "I'm not here for a reunion, Avery."

He pushed off the wall with a scoff, brushing imaginary dust from his sleeves. "Then you're here for war."

Aazar didn't respond right away. Her mind flicked back to the facility: the humans in the chairs, the hum of machines that didn't care who they killed so long as they harvested what they wanted.

"I'm here because what I saw was wrong."

Avery tilted his head, curiosity flickering in his gaze. "You mean the machine? Caleb didn't even try to hide it?"

"No. He walked me through it like it was a tour of a wine cellar. Explained everything with a smile. Like the death of those people was the price of innovation."

"It is," Avery said simply. "To them. To the Legacies."

Aazar folded her arms, jaw tight. "You were right about them."

Avery took a step forward, his voice lowering, almost a whisper. "Say it again."

His tone made her skin crawl. She glared at him. "You were right. But don't make me say it a third time."

Avery smiled like she'd given him the best compliment he'd received all year. "Then let's burn it all down."

Aazar stepped back, her body bristling. "I'm not rejoining The Order. I'm not interested in building a throne of bones."

"You think I care why you help me?" Avery shot back, his smile fading. "I just care that you do. We both want the same thing now."

She hesitated, the weight of his words pressing on her. She hated that he was right. Again.

"We can strike the outer wall first," Avery said, already pulling up a hologram from a palm-sized device. "My team can trigger the emergency response, draw out their enforcers. You'll have a ten-minute window to get in and plant charges at the base of the storage chamber or overload the machine. Take out the core, and the entire system collapses."

Aazar studied the projection. "And the humans?"

"Collateral," Avery replied coldly. "Most are too far gone. You saw them. That machine takes more than it gives."

Her stomach twisted. "We get as many out as we can."

Avery rolled his eyes, but didn't fight her on it. "Fine. But we move in three days."

She turned without a word.

* * *

Back at the house, the mood was suffocating. The tension in the air was palpable. The group hadn't recovered from their last encounter with Avery, and Aazar could feel the fractures widening. KJ barely looked up when she passed him in the hallway. Monica watched her too closely. Simon had a twitch in his jaw that he hadn't had a week ago.

In the kitchen, Monica cornered her.

"Where did you go?"

"Supplies."

"You don't have any bags."

Aazar paused. "Didn't need much."

Monica didn't believe her. She didn't say so, but her silence said it all.

Later that night, KJ passed her in the hall. She opened her mouth, but he kept walking. No nod. No glance. Nothing.

When the house finally went still, Aazar stood outside Monica's door for a long time before knocking. She expected silence, but he called out, "It's open."

She stepped inside. Monica lay in bed, watching a television show on her phone.

"Can't sleep?" she asked.

"Can you?"

She sat in the chair beside his bed. "No."

Monica didn't blame her. But she didn't comfort her either. She didn't have to. That made it worse.

"My parents don't remember me." Monica offered suddenly.

Aazar blinked a few times, but stayed silent.

"They never really paid any attention to me in the first place," Monica said. "Mom was too busy gambling at the racetrack, and Dad was too busy at his corporate office."

Aazar frowned as Monica continued.

"I didn't blame them for not noticing that I had changed. Then one day, I realized I would be better off if I let them go. There was no point in fighting for their attention anymore, so I made it easy for all of us. I took their memories of me, packed a bag, and never looked back."

Monica looked at her.

"This war you keep walking toward," she said, "you think you can win it?"

Aazar looked at her hands. "I think I have to try."

She nodded. "Just… don't forget why you started."

Aazar left without another word.

Back in her room, a new resolve built itself from the bones of her shame and regret. Avery thought she was a threat. The Legacies had used her. Caleb had lied. The world was folding in on itself, and someone had to stand up.

If they wanted her to be dangerous, she would become a weapon.

Not for Avery.

Not for Caleb.

For the ones who couldn't fight back.

Aazar stared at her reflection in the dark windowpane.

Truth

Aazar stood before her group: Simon, Monica, Hugo, Flenoid, and the others: each face tense with anticipation.

"We need to talk," Aazar said finally, her voice slicing through the silence. "About what I saw in the rehabilitation center."

The others slowly gathered around her in a tight semi-circle in the candle-lit living room. The hum of the generators was the only sound besides the steady beat of her heart thumping in her ears.

"It wasn't a rehab center," she said, her voice steady. "It was a harvesting facility."

Gasps filled the room. Flenoid remained still, his gaze unreadable.

"They have a machine," Aazar continued. "One that mines human consciousness. It extracts thoughts, memories, and emotions. Every fear, every joy. Converts them into data for the Legacy Variants to control humans."

Monica's mouth fell open. Simon looked like he might be sick. Hugo crossed his arms, eyes narrowing in disbelief.

"Are you sure?" he asked, his voice tight. "You saw it with your own eyes?"

"I saw people hooked up to machines. I saw them die, one by one, as their minds were stripped bare. Caleb explained it to me like it was nothing. Like it was necessary."

"Why didn't you destroy it?" Hugo demanded, frustration creeping into his voice.

"Because I was alone," she snapped, temper flaring. "And Caleb would've known it was me. I had to act like I was okay with it. Like I was just another loyal bodyguard."

Hugo scoffed and turned away. Simon placed a calming hand on her shoulder.

"So, what now?" Monica asked, her voice tight. "We can't let this continue."

"We won't," Aazar said. "But this changes everything. We have to align with The Order and take them out."

"The Order?" Hugo yelled, "After everything they did to us last time? How can we trust them?"

"We have no choice," Aazar said. "We need the manpower. And the spies. We need to unify with more Variants than we know right now."

Monica nodded as she looked up. "I'm in. We need all the help we can get. Those Legacy guys are scary."

Simon nodded. "I'm in too."

Monica failed to hide the small smile on her face.

Logan raised a hand. "Same."

Hugo huffed loudly. Aazar rounded on him.

"We can't treat the Legacy Variants like just another political enemy." She said. "They're not just corrupt. They're predatory."

Hugo looked over his shoulder, his gaze skeptical. "And you want to take them on? To save a bunch of Normies? After everything Flenoid said and everything you've seen?"

"I'm trying to fix it," Aazar replied.

"Are you? Because it feels like you're just reacting. Like you keep getting caught off guard."

Simon stepped forward. "That's not fair. She's been leading all of us while carrying the weight of every mistake."

"That's the problem!" Hugo snapped. "She carries everything alone, makes all the decisions, and expects us to follow. She's no better than The Order at this point."

The silence that followed was suffocating.

* * *

The next morning, the house was quiet. Most of the group had scattered to different corners, watching television or playing card games. Aazar made coffee in silence, her jaw sore from clenching it all night.

She felt his presence before she heard his footsteps.

KJ.

He stood in the doorway, sleep still in his eyes, a hoodie hanging off his frame like a ghost.

She braced herself. But instead of bitterness, his face showed something closer to concern.

"You okay?"

"Yeah. You?"

He nodded, grabbed a chipped mug from the counter, and filled it with coffee before sitting across from her. Silence settled between them.

"I'm sorry," she said, her voice low.

He didn't respond.

"I should've told you about Caleb and Johnny. About the machine."

Still nothing. Aazar sat down across from him, the chair creaking beneath her.

"I was scared."

That made him look up.

"I didn't want you to look at me the way you did when I told you about Avery. I didn't want to lose that version of us."

KJ blinked slowly. "That version doesn't exist. Not anymore."

Her chest ached. "Then what are we?"

He hesitated. "Trying."

They sat in silence.

Then KJ reached across the table and took her hand. His thumb brushed over her knuckles.

"I hated you for shutting me out," he said, his voice soft. "But I hate the idea of losing you more."

Tears welled up in her eyes.

"I want to be better," she whispered.

"Then be better," he said, voice low.

The air felt lighter after that, though silence still hung between them.

"Have you dealt with the Caleb fiasco?"

She met his gaze. "He apologized for the pool party. But not for the machine. That part… he was proud of."

KJ turned the chipped mug in his hands, his eyes focused on the motion. "Are you still working for him?"

She shook her head. "Not anymore. Now that I see what they're hiding, I can't be a part of that kind of business."

He nodded slowly. Then KJ reached out, gently brushing a curl behind her ear. "So what now?"

She took a deep breath. "Now we stop pretending they aren't a threat. We find the machine. We burn it to the ground. And we make the Legacy Variants wish they'd never touched a human mind."

KJ's smile sharpened. "There's the Aazar I know."

She reached for his hand. He didn't pull away.

And for the first time in weeks, she let herself believe that maybe they still had a chance.

Later that night, she stood on the balcony outside her room, wind tugging at her curls. The city lights glimmered in the distance, but they felt like another world.

Behind her, the sliding door opened.

KJ stepped out, wrapping a blanket around his shoulders. He didn't speak, just leaned beside her.

For a while, they just listened to the wind.

"Do you believe in redemption?" she asked.

KJ didn't answer right away. "I believe in choices. In trying again. Even if it hurts."

She turned her head. "Even if it means forgiving someone who broke your heart for the greater good?"

He looked at her. "Especially then."

"Do you think about Todd and what we did to him?" Aazar asked.

KJ was quiet for a moment. "I feel guilty about leaving him, but he left us with no choice. I'm a little upset at how nice things have been without him around, but I would fix things with him in a heartbeat if I could. I still love him."

In the quiet, something began to knit itself back together. Not perfectly. Not all at once. But enough to breathe.

KJ stood up after a few minutes. "Well, I'm going in; it's freezing out here."

"It's not that bad," Aazar said.

"Well, you run pretty hot." He said. "Maybe it's the fire thing."

She smiled despite herself. "You go ahead. I'll go inside later."

He kissed her gently on the forehead and walked back into the house as Aazar stared out at the glimmering lights of the city.

And in the house below them, Hugo sat at the edge of his bed, staring at the communicator hidden in his drawer. The screen blinked once, then faded to black.

* * *

"You didn't sleep."

Aazar woke with a start and looked around. She'd accidentally fallen asleep on the bench outside. She blinked at the rising sun coming over the horizon, creating a silhouette of the city below. KJ was looking at her with a small smile on his face from the sliding glass door.

"I did!" Aazar exclaimed as she stretched. " At least for a few hours. Did you sleep?"

He gave a small, humorless laugh. "Barely."

She turned to face him as she rubbed the sleep from her eyes. "KJ... last night: what you said. I meant it too. I don't want to keep shutting you out."

His eyes flicked to her, tired and guarded. "But you do."

The words weren't angry. They were just... resigned. That hurt more.

She took a step closer. "I'm trying to change that."

KJ leaned against the frame of the door, his arms folding over his chest. "I know. But every time I start to feel close again, something pulls you away. War. Secrets. Guilt. It's like there's always something between us, Aazar. Always."

She blinked against the sting in her eyes. "I'm scared that if you saw all of it: what I've done, what I'm still capable of doing: you'd walk away."

"I won't walk," he said softly as he sat beside her. "But I won't stand in place, either. Not if I'm not really in this with you."

Aazar moved closer to him. She reached for KJ's hand, her fingers brushing over his. For a heartbeat, he didn't move. Then, slowly, he turned his palm to meet hers.

"You are," she said. "You always have been."

He let out a shaky breath. "Then let me stay."

They stood like that, still and quiet, their hands clasped gently between them. It wasn't forgiveness, not entirely. But it was a step. A shared breath. A promise to try.

"Come on, we've got to go. Everyone's waiting."

Camp

They stepped out of the house and onto the porch to join the others. Monica sat on the steps beside Simon, their shoulders brushing in the quiet comfort they'd found together. Hugo stood off to the side, arms crossed, his expression unreadable.

Aazar and KJ stood by the door for a moment, watching them in silence. She almost didn't want to ruin the morning with a drive into the desert for a meeting with Avery and his group.

"Morning," Aazar said softly, her voice barely rising above the breeze.

Monica gave a tired smile. "You look like hell."

"Feels accurate." Aazar moved past them, heading toward the small rise at the edge of the yard. From there, she spotted a patrol car driving down the street..

The group began piling into the rented van, packing tents, sleeping bags, and snacks for the trip. Simon slammed the door shut and jumped into the front seat. Aazar had a flashback to when she had boarded a bus headed for the Order camp years ago. The more things change, the more they stay the same.

KJ interrupted her thoughts with a simple truth.

"The others are expecting something. A plan. Direction."

Aazar turned to face him. "They'll get one."

He reached out, brushing a stray curl behind her ear. His fingers lingered just a second too long.

"We need to show The Order we're united. That we're something solid,"

KJ said, his voice steady. "Otherwise, Avery will pick us off one by one."

She wondered how much of that was about the mission: and how much was about their relationship.

"Then let's show them how strong we are," she said, her tone firm.

The desert morning was cooler than expected. They reached the meeting point: a dilapidated water treatment plant nestled between California and Arizona. Dry winds rolled over the cracked pavement, rusted fences humming with occasional gusts. Aazar stood at the edge of the crumbling lot, arms crossed, as two vans approached from opposite directions.

One was her group: Simon, Monica, KJ, and Flenoid: tense and silent. The other, smaller and sleeker, unmistakably belonged to The Order. Their figures stepped out in muted grays and worn utility gear, dressed for war but unwilling to admit it. They had ditched the classic red look once they started taking over cities.

From the moment The Order's boots hit the ground, the air turned brittle. Every step toward one another felt like an aftershock. Uneasy hands hovered near hidden weapons. Trust, if it existed at all, was fragile.

Avery emerged from the back of The Order's van, cloaked in that all-too-familiar calm. His coat swept in the wind, his posture arrogant, magnetic. His eyes locked onto Aazar with that same knowing smirk: one she used to love, then fear, then hate.

"Aazar," he said.

"Avery," she returned, her voice as sharp as flint.

As Aazar scanned the group of Order members Avery had brought, her eyes landed on two figures behind him. Her stomach tightened.

Lizzie grinned, as always: same over-sized boots, same effortless defiance in her stance, hands stuffed into her jacket pockets. Beside her stood Nessa, taller now, leaner, but with the same sharp, guarded eyes Aazar remembered from years ago. Guilt surged through Aazar for leaving without a word. Nessa actively avoided her gaze.

Lizzie's grin widened when their eyes met. "Well, if it isn't the woman of the hour."

"Didn't realize you were still playing soldier," Aazar said flatly.

"Funny. Didn't realize you were still playing leader," Lizzie muttered, arms crossed.

Avery didn't intervene. If anything, he seemed entertained.

KJ walked up beside Aazar and pressed a kiss to her temple. The gesture, subtle but calculated, hit its target. Avery's smirk flickered. Lizzie's smile faded.

"Let's get started," Aazar said, pulling away from KJ and nodding toward a nearby building. "We have work to do."

Inside, a makeshift table made of scrap wood and cinder blocks had been set up. Flenoid had insisted on using ancient tech, and Avery seemed to take pleasure in the large map of the western corridor spread out across it, marked with red ink, highlighters, and torn post-its. The setup was cumbersome, but Flenoid was determined to keep his intel offline: holographs could be easily hacked.

The Order's team stood across from Aazar's group, the rift between them almost palpable.

"We need to move fast," Aazar said, planting her palms on the table. "The facility isn't just protected by tech. We're talking layered Variant security, AI surveillance, and electromagnetic field barriers."

"They're harvesting people," Simon added, his voice tight. "We can't waste time."

Avery gave a small, acknowledging nod. "Agreed. We hit the neural core first. If we can take that out, the machine will lose processing speed."

Flenoid stepped forward, his eyes narrowed beneath his hood. "And the power source?"

"Here," Lizzie pointed to the far western wing on the map. "It's isolated with the machine. If we disable it, the extraction process will stall. But we'll only have a few minutes before they reboot from the auxiliary node. You'd need to overpower the machine before that."

"What about the humans," Monica asked.

"The humans probably won't survive, but the destruction of the machine will keep the Legacies from attacking anymore for a while."

Aazar was about to respond when something shifted in the air: just enough for Flenoid to notice. His gaze drifted toward the back wall, where Hugo had been moments before.

He was gone.

Flenoid subtly motioned toward Aazar. She followed his gaze.

"Hugo," she said sharply, stepping away from the table.

No response.

Monica caught the cue immediately.

"Go," Aazar whispered.

Monica was already moving, slipping through the shadows like smoke.

Back at the table, Avery watched her carefully.

"Trouble?" he asked, far too amused.

Aazar didn't look at him. "Not yet."

The planning resumed, but something had shifted. The enemy wasn't just in the machines. The enemy might be among them.

And that meant Aazar couldn't afford to hesitate: not again.

Traitors

Aazar sat alone at the shaded table near the edge of the dusty field where they'd set up a temporary shelter for the summit. The Arizona sun filtered through the mesh tarp above her, casting shifting patterns on the surface of the wood. She picked absently at the crust of her sandwich, the lack of appetite sharp in its familiarity. The meeting earlier that morning had been tense, to say the least. And Hugo disappearing mid-meeting certainly hadn't helped her case in front of Avery.

The Order and her group had huddled over maps, arguing about entry points and supply chains. Every sentence was thick with suspicion. She didn't blame them: she felt the same. They were strangers in ideology, even if they shared an enemy.

Aazar watched Avery, laughing easily with Lizzie and Nessa as they ate. He had never been this personable when they'd been together. I guess you don't brood in your tent anymore, she thought despite herself.

She was halfway through picking apart her sandwich when KJ dropped into the chair beside her. His brow was glistening with sweat, his arms crossed, unsure if this was a check-in or a confrontation.

"You okay?" he asked quietly.

Aazar gave him a small nod, eyes still on the table. "Just tired."

"You barely touched your food."

"Food doesn't solve everything."

"No," KJ said, his voice softening. "But it helps."

Before Aazar could respond, Lizzie's voice sliced through the murmuring field like a whip.

"Looking a little flamed out right now," Lizzie drawled, strutting up in her too-clean boots, a sharp grin in place. "Still pretending you know what you're doing?"

"*Flamed out?*" Aazar's lip curled. "That was corny."

"Just saying," Lizzie continued, plopping down on the edge of the table. "People follow leaders because they believe in them. Not because they're scared, or because they don't know what else to do. How long do you think you can hold this mess together?"

Before Aazar could retort, Avery appeared behind Lizzie and gave her a single look. She quieted, but not before raising her hands in mock surrender and strolling off with an exaggerated sway.

Avery turned to Aazar. "Walk with me?"

KJ shot him a look, but Avery ignored it.

Aazar rose silently, nodding to KJ that she'd be fine.

Aazar and Avery walked a few paces away from the group, the desert air still, thick with unspoken words. She kept her back straight, her focus ahead, though she could feel the weight of his gaze on her.

Avery's voice broke the silence first, quiet and steady. "You know, the short hair is growing on me. I didn't like it at first, but I think it suits you, Aazar."

She didn't look at him, but her pulse quickened at the compliment. The way he said her name, like it was something only he could say, still made her skin prickle.

"Compliments won't work, Avery. I'm not the same naive person I was when I met you," she said flatly, eyes fixed on the cracked earth beneath her boots. "Neither are you."

Avery let out a soft laugh, low and rich, but it lacked the warmth it once had. "No, you're right. We've both changed." He took a breath, his tone turning serious. "But I remember who you were. Who we were."

Aazar stiffened, but didn't respond. The words hung there between them, heavy and loaded. She couldn't afford to go back to that place, couldn't afford to let him pull her into the past.

"You're still angry," Avery observed, watching her closely. "I can't believe you destroyed my base, and you're the one who's holding a grudge."

Aazar clenched her jaw. "You're not innocent, Avery. You're a liar and a manipulator. You destroyed any trust we could've had with each other."

He stopped walking, turning to face her, the sharpness in his gaze matching her own. "You think I'm worse than the people we're fighting? You're wrong." He stepped closer, voice softening, but there was a coldness underneath. "I did what I did because I cared about our people. I always cared about you. Don't you remember?"

The memories flooded in, unbidden. The nights in dark corners of their shared apartment, whispers of dreams and promises. The way he'd held her, whispered her name like he meant it.

"I remember," she said quietly. "I remember how you used to protect me. How you made me feel safe. But I also remember the way you started to change. The way you-" Her voice faltered, a tightness in her chest making it hard to breathe. "The way you drugged our people. How you worked with the enemy to do it. You made me believe you loved me, that I mattered to you, only to throw me away when it suited you."

Avery's expression shifted, hurt flashing briefly before his usual mask fell back into place. "You don't understand, Aazar. I thought I was saving us all."

Aazar looked at him, searching his eyes for any hint of sincerity, any trace of the person she once loved. But all she saw was a man who had buried himself beneath layers of power and control.

"You didn't save me, Avery," she said, her voice thick with frustration. "You destroyed everything we had. And now you're asking me to, what, forget all of that?"

Avery took a step closer, his voice barely above a whisper. "We were good together. I know I messed up, but I still think there's something between us. Something we can fix."

Aazar almost laughed in his face, stepping back as the familiar sting of old wounds resurfaced. "I can't go back there. I've fought too hard to get away from the person I was with you. You were my world, Avery. But you destroyed that world, piece by piece."

His gaze softened for a moment, almost as if he were remembering the same things, but it quickly hardened again, the mask falling back into place. "I know you hate me for what I did. But you can't pretend you didn't feel something too. You can't just erase everything we were."

Aazar's breath hitched, but she steadied herself. "I'm not erasing anything. But I've learned. I've learned that I can't keep letting people like you control my life. Not anymore."

Avery stepped back, his jaw tightening. "Maybe you've forgotten what it was like to be with me. Maybe you've moved on. But I haven't. I haven't forgotten what you meant to me."

Her heart twisted painfully. There was still a part of her that wanted to believe him. She wanted to be the kind of girl who could fall so deeply in love again. But she couldn't. Not with him. Not after everything.

As Aazar turned away, she felt a strange emptiness in her chest, but maybe that was for the better.

"She's not wrong, you know," Avery said.

Aazar looked at him, confused. "Who are you talking about?"

"Lizzie."

She rolled her eyes. "About which part? The insults or the smugness?"

He smirked. "Leadership. It's not about knowing all the answers. It's about making the hard calls, even when they hate you for it."

"I know that."

"Do you?" Avery tilted his head. "Because from what I've seen, you're still trying to be everything to everyone. Do you want their love or their loyalty? Pick one."

Aazar bristled. "I'm not like you."

"And that's why they'll break you," Avery replied calmly. "Because you care too much about being understood."

"I thought I understood you," Aazar said, her voice low.

Before Avery could respond, KJ stormed across the field, his eyes locked on Avery.

"You need help, Aazar?" KJ asked, not bothering to mask the edge in his voice.

Aazar clenched her jaw. "I'm fine. We're just talking."

KJ glanced between them, his gaze lingering a moment too long. "Didn't look like just talking."

"I said I'm fine," she repeated, sharper this time. "Go cool off."

KJ's face pinched with frustration. He hesitated, then turned and walked away without another word.

Avery let out a slow whistle. "Protective. But impulsive."

"Don't start," she said, the irritation clear in her voice.

"Just saying," he murmured, his tone softer now. "It used to be me you'd snap at like that. I still think about that night, you know. The last time we: "

"Don't," Aazar cut him off, voice firm. "That version of us is gone."

Avery studied her for a long moment. Then, to her relief, he nodded.

Suddenly. Monica appeared, her breathing quick and face set in a serious expression.

"It's Hugo," she said. "He left to call Johnny."

Aazar's stomach dropped. "Are you sure?"

Monica nodded. "I erased his memory before he could call. He doesn't remember anything from this morning. He dropped the phone after. The contact, Johnny, was the screen."

"Where is he now?"

"I led him to the bus and told him to wait for you. He seemed confused, trying to figure out what happened."

Aazar nodded.

Avery raised an eyebrow. "You still sure you don't want my advice on who to trust?"

Aazar didn't respond. She simply turned and walked back toward camp, the fire in her chest burning steady but now laced with betrayal.

Erased Child

The path to the van felt like a quiet, weighted moment. Aazar walked ahead, her arms tightly wrapped across her stomach. The wind tugged at the hem of her jacket, lifting loose strands of hair across her cheek, but she didn't brush them away. The world had narrowed to the sound of her boots on the gravel and the deep thrum of her heart, steady but heavy.

Hugo sat on the steps of the old rented van, dazed, his elbows resting on his knees as he traced the thread of his sleeve with an absent stare. Monica had done her work well, but Hugo looked as though he had been lost somewhere in between waking and sleeping, disconnected, like someone who had been pulled from the edge of a dream.

Aazar took in a slow breath as she approached, her eyes on the ground, but the weight in her chest only grew heavier with each step. She almost didn't want to ruin the moment with a confrontation. Not yet. Not like this. She had barely processed everything else, let alone Hugo's betrayal.

"Hey," Aazar said, her voice carrying the distance between them.

Hugo looked up, his face softening as he recognized her. "Oh, hey, Z," he said, his voice quieter than usual. "I was just waiting here, like Monica said. Everything okay?"

Aazar stood there for a moment, silent, her gaze fixed on him. She didn't answer immediately. She didn't know how to. "What do you remember from this morning?"

Hugo blinked, his brow furrowing. "Uh… not much. We were talking about the meeting, and then... I don't know. It's like I just blacked out, and here I am."

She studied him closely. Something was off. His energy was disjointed, like the fabric of his thoughts had been pulled apart. He didn't look at her directly, his gaze lingering on the hem of his sleeve, as if trying to anchor himself to something solid. The way he was twisting the fabric reminded her of someone trying to hold on to their own reality.

"Do you remember who you were going to call?" Aazar asked, watching him carefully.

Hugo frowned, brow creasing. "What?"

"You left to make a call. Monica stopped you. Do you remember who you were calling?"

There was a flicker in his eyes. Something almost remembered. He opened his mouth, closed it again, and swallowed hard.

"I... don't know," he stammered, voice trembling slightly.

Aazar stepped closer. Her shadow fell across him, the space between them growing thick with tension.

"It was Johnny," she said, her voice steady but cutting through the quiet.

Hugo's face froze, his eyes wide with confusion. "What? No... I wouldn't."

"You were going to call Johnny," she said again, this time her voice harder.

Silence hung between them for a long moment, until finally, Hugo exhaled, his breath shaky. "I didn't tell him everything. Just enough. Enough to make him think I was still useful, in case things went south with you and Avery."

Aazar's chest tightened. "You betrayed us."

"No," he said quickly, rising to his feet. "I wasn't trying to betray anyone. I was trying to keep everyone safe. You think this alliance with Avery will last? You think Caleb's not just waiting for the right moment to stab you in the back? You keep dragging us into this war like we're soldiers, not friends."

"We are in a war," she snapped, stepping closer. "And I never asked you to follow me."

"You didn't have to," Hugo replied bitterly. "We followed you because we believed in you. But you keep secrets. You hide things and make decisions without telling us. That's not leadership. That's manipulation."

Aazar's jaw tightened. The words echoed in her head. She had just said something similar to Avery. The weight of Hugo's words, the sting, made her feel exposed.

But still, Hugo had made his choice. He had called Johnny, and there was no going back.

"You can't stay," Aazar said, her voice final. "Not with us. Not anymore."

Hugo flinched, as if struck. He looked at her for a long, silent moment before his shoulders slumped. He nodded once and stepped back.

Aazar didn't look back as she turned toward the others. The space between them had stretched further than she ever expected.

The group had gathered just outside the bus, their faces tight with anxiety. Aazar, still trying to catch her breath, stood before them, knowing what she had to say but dreading the fallout.

"Hugo was feeding information to Johnny," she said quietly, her voice cold.

A few gasps rippled through the group. Simon's face darkened, and Monica's expression was unreadable. Hugo's betrayal stung deeper now that it was out in the open.

"I erased his memory before he could tell him anything useful," Monica said, her voice tight but resolute.

Flenoid nodded from the back of the group, his gaze somber. "These fractures were inevitable. The closer we get to the center, the more pressure we'll feel."

Avery, ever the opportunist, sauntered into the group, arms crossed, his smile broad and calculating. "Tough gig, isn't it? Leadership. Everyone wants to be close to the fire until they feel the burn."

KJ shot him a dark look, but Aazar stopped him with a hand.

"Don't," she said, her tone low but firm.

Avery shrugged, his grin never fading. "Just saying. Leading's harder than it looks."

Aazar turned back to the group, shaking off the discomfort Avery's words triggered. There was no time for distractions now.

The sun was dipping low on the horizon, casting long orange shadows over the gravel lot beside the van. Hugo sat on the edge of the seat, hands clenched in his lap, his face vacant.

Aazar stepped forward, her boots ringing out against the floor. Hugo blinked up at her, confusion and disorientation etched on his face.

"Hey," he said, voice weak. "You said to wait here…? I: sorry, I feel off. Like I lost time."

"You did," Aazar said softly, her gaze piercing.

KJ stepped beside her. "Tell him again."

Aazar hesitated. The words stung, but they needed to be said. "You tried to contact Johnny."

Hugo's expression crumbled into confusion. "What? No, no, I wouldn't: why would I do that?"

"Because you turned on us," Simon said, his voice hard as stone.

The group shifted, murmuring among themselves. The atmosphere became electric with tension.

"We have to make a decision," Flenoid said, stepping forward. "We can't have a spy in our ranks."

"I agree," Aazar said, her voice unwavering.

Hugo's face flushed with panic. "Wait… I don't remember doing that. I didn't mean to betray anyone. I: Monica erased it, right? How do you know all this?"

"You were seen dialing," Monica replied. "And I felt your panic. You knew what you were doing."

KJ crossed his arms. "So what? We exile him? Toss him out into the wild like he never mattered?"

"He put us all in danger," Simon snapped. "We barely survived a fight with The Order. What if next time it's worse when we face the Legacies?"

"He doesn't remember," Monica repeated, but there was no conviction in her voice.

"And next time, he might not be so sloppy," Flenoid added, his voice sharp. "You all want to give him a second chance, but how many more do we survive?"

Aazar felt the burn of frustration rising in her chest. The group was splintering again. She was stuck in the middle of it, fighting for something that might be already lost.

Flenoid's voice broke through the noise. "Leadership is deciding what others can't. This is your call."

Aazar took a long, steadying breath. She couldn't delay the decision any longer. The group was watching her, waiting for the final word. Avery looked on, curious about her decision.

She walked up to Hugo, her eyes meeting his with an intensity he couldn't look away from.

"I believe you were weak. Not malicious. But weakness can still destroy us."

He trembled at her words, his shoulders sagging.

Aazar turned to Monica. "Do it."

Monica hesitated, then nodded. "He won't remember us. He won't remember anything beyond being found in the desert."

KJ winced. Simon's eyes were closed, pained. Flenoid was silent, arms folded across his chest, watching with heavy eyes.

Monica placed her fingers gently on Hugo's temples. Avery, who had been standing off to the side, slipped his hands into his pockets and walked back inside the base.

The air felt different now, the weight of the decision hanging heavily in the air. Aazar didn't know what would come next, but she knew they couldn't keep making excuses. The choice was made.

Band of Brothers

The wind rattled the edges of the temporary tents, and morale was at an all-time low. News of Hugo's betrayal had spread like wildfire, and the tension between both groups was thick enough to cut with a knife. Aazar stood at the center of it all, flanked by KJ and Simon, with Flenoid not far behind.

Another van pulled up, and Aazar's jaw dropped when she saw who jumped out.

Todd had arrived. He walked beside another Variant from The Order, but a few steps behind, like a tethered shadow. His hair was longer than Aazar remembered, tucked into a low ponytail. His face was paler too, more hollowed out than when they last crossed paths.

But KJ noticed none of that. The moment Todd stepped into view, KJ's jaw clenched. Aazar felt him stiffen beside her.

"I wasn't sure you'd come," KJ said, his voice low, trying for calm but failing.

Todd stopped a few feet away, eyes glinting. "I almost didn't."

The wind pushed between them, carrying sand and silence.

"You look like shit," KJ said.

"You look like a traitor," Todd replied, not even blinking.

Aazar stepped slightly forward, but KJ raised a hand to stop her. "Don't."

"Yeah, don't, KJ," Todd mocked her. "I just wanted to see if your new life was worth risking your life for." He turned his glare to Aazar. "Again."

KJ's jaw clenched. "This isn't about her."

Todd scoffed. "It's always about her. Ever since you met her, you dropped everything else. The Order. Me."

Aazar stiffened, but didn't speak. KJ looked like he wanted to yell, but instead, he just muttered, "I didn't drop you. I just chose something else for once."

"You chose someone who tears everything apart," Todd snapped.

"I tried to protect you my whole life."

"Yeah, and then you abandoned me."

KJ's shoulders dropped. "I didn't know how to help you anymore, Todd. You wouldn't let me."

"I was drowning. You swam away."

Before KJ could respond, Flenoid stepped between them. "Now is not the time. There are bigger things at stake than your family drama."

Todd looked like he might argue, but instead, he turned sharply and walked into the base. Aazar, Flenoid, and KJ followed him. Todd took a seat near the far end of the table.

With a sigh, Aazar moved to the center of the table. "Let's get back on track. We've got a target and limited time. This facility isn't just housing civilians. It's running the machines. The ones pulling memories and emotions from human minds."

She glanced around the table. Everyone was watching her, but not everyone was with her. Simon and Monica sat close, clearly on her side. Lizzie leaned back with her arms crossed, eyes narrowed. Todd looked bored. Hugo sat near the back, dazed and confused.

Monica leaned in and whispered something to Simon, who nodded. Aazar caught the exchange but let it go.

She continued. "We need a direct team to infiltrate and disable the core of the machine. That means going in fast, clean, and quiet. We don't have enough firepower to fight off whatever protection the Legacy Variants have stashed there. We need a strategy."

Avery, leaning against the wall, finally spoke up. "I'll send in three from my side. Lizzie, Nessa, and Todd. You pick three from yours."

Aazar gave him a tight nod. "Simon, Monica, and myself."

"We hit them fast and hard," Avery said. "We'll divide the work into two groups. One to destroy the machines, the other to cover the exit."

"Won't that trigger a lockdown?" Monica asked, arms crossed tightly.

"Yes," Aazar said. "That's why I'm going in first."

KJ frowned. "No, we go in together."

"You'll be with the strike team," Aazar replied. "But someone has to draw fire. That's me."

"You're not a martyr."

"I'm not. I'm the most dangerous one here. They know me."

Simon spoke up. "Then they'll expect you. That's a disadvantage."

"Not if we make them think I'm alone," Aazar countered. "It buys us seconds. That's all we'll need."

There were nods, murmurs of agreement. Even Avery didn't object. Aazar looked at the faces around her. Some old, some new. Some still unsure if they could trust her. Maybe they couldn't.

Later that night, KJ found Aazar standing alone, staring at the fire pit behind the camp.

"He's not wrong," she said as KJ approached.

"Todd?"

She nodded. "You did leave him."

KJ exhaled, long and tired. "I know. But I didn't know how to stay either. Everything back then felt like quicksand."

Aazar looked up at him, the fire reflecting in her eyes. "You could fix it now. If you tried."

He studied her, then the shadows beyond the fire. "Maybe I will."

They stood in silence, the night humming around them.

"Are you scared?" he asked.

"Yes."

"Good," he said. "Means you still care what happens."

She turned to him. "Do you?"

He didn't answer right away. "More than you know."

And then he walked away, back into the dark.

Leaving her with her fear.

Adrift

She stood alone in the middle of a barren field, the air thick with ash falling like snow from a sky too heavy to breathe under. The ground beneath her was scorched, cracked open like the earth had been seared from within. Faint, red seams glowed where the earth seemed to pulse with its own unnatural heat. All around her, the charred remnants of grass reached toward the sky, skeletal and brittle, stretching like fingers of some forgotten ghost.

She turned, slowly, her eyes squinting against the smoke.

"Mom?" Her voice barely cut through the crackling air, swallowed by the weight of the silence.

A figure appeared in the distance, walking with a slow, deliberate grace. It was her mother: dignified, sharp-eyed, proud. Her dark curls tumbled into a braid, her dress simple but regal, a shadow of the woman she used to know.

Aazar's breath hitched. She took a step forward, and something soft caught in her throat.

"I need your help," she whispered, the words barely there. "Please. I don't know who I am anymore. I don't know if I'm doing the right thing."

Her mother's steps faltered, her eyes hardening, cold.

Then, without warning, flames erupted around her mother's form, swallowing the distance between them. Her skin cracked open, burning light spilling through the fissures as she lunged toward Aazar.

Instinctively, Aazar raised her hands, the fire building in her chest, but her limbs felt heavy. Stone. The flames that had once surged through her effortlessly refused to rise.

"You're not my daughter," her mother hissed, her voice venomous, ripping through the dream.

Aazar screamed-

... and jerked upright in bed, heart pounding, drenched in sweat. The room was still. Quiet. The faint sound of KJ's breathing from the couch was the only thing that anchored her back to reality.

She pressed her palms into her eyes, trying to steady her breath, to still the trembling in her chest. Her body was a taut string, pulled too tight. Her mind scrambled, fragments of the dream clawing their way to the surface.

Her mother's gaze. Her voice. The flames.

Even if it was only a dream, it had left a crack in her resolve. She wasn't sure if it was guilt or fear that crawled up her spine.

Outside, the sky was still dark, the world holding its breath. But Aazar stood anyway, unable to sleep again.

The house felt quieter than usual, even for the late afternoon. The hallway was empty, the sounds of laughter and feet scuffling nowhere to be found. Only the soft creak of old floorboards echoed, the low hum of unease pulsing in the background. Aazar sat by the window, her eyes fixed on the dust motes dancing in a lone beam of light that cut through the room. Outside, the world went on, unaware of how close everything had come to shattering the night before.

They had decided to go back to the city, at least for now. Aazar wanted them all to have a chance to rest, to sleep in their own beds before the battle came. It felt strange: like time was slipping through her fingers. She thought of how young they all were. She remembered her first battle, just seventeen, thinking she was ready. But she had no idea what she was really up against.

* * *

Hours later, Logan was sitting in the middle of the living room, leg in a brace, surrounded by three younger teens who fidgeted nervously.

"No, no, no," Logan said, raising a hand, exasperated. "You don't channel

115

power by scrunching your face and hoping for the best. It's not a bowel movement, it's a breath."

One of the boys, Benji, stifled a laugh, then gave it another try. His palms flickered, glowing faintly, before sputtering out like a dying ember.

"Better," Logan nodded, sweat gathering on his forehead. He gripped the arms of his chair, his breath shallow. "Again."

Aazar watched from the hallway, her chest tight, her heart clenching. Logan was still adjusting to the aftermath of the last battle. His body wasn't fully healed yet, but he never complained. He just kept pushing himself, kept trying.

In the kitchen, Monica and Simon stood side by side, leaning over a steaming pot of tea. Their hands brushed, again and again, like some unspoken bond between them. Simon laughed softly at something Monica whispered, and she smirked, pressing a joint between her fingers with practiced ease.

"You're a terrible influence," Simon teased, but he didn't move away.

"And yet you haven't left," Monica replied, voice soft, but laced with something that made Simon pause.

"You know," Simon said, glancing at her, "I don't want to be anywhere else."

Aazar turned away from the scene, her chest tight with something she couldn't name.

She walked out to the back porch where KJ sat on the old bench, his head tilted toward the sky, eyes closed. Without a word, Aazar sat beside him, the weight of the night lingering between them.

"Monica's gotten better at controlling her power," KJ said, his voice barely more than a murmur.

Aazar nodded. "She's more grounded now."

KJ sighed, looking out at the empty horizon. "So is everyone. Even me, I think."

The silence between them was heavy, but not uncomfortable. Just… real.

"I keep thinking about Logan," Aazar said quietly. "About what he lost."

KJ's gaze shifted toward her, his expression unreadable. "He's not broken."

"No," she said, voice small. "But I should've protected him."

"You always say that."

"Because it's always true."

KJ turned toward her fully now, his eyes soft. "You can't protect everyone. But you still try. That's what makes you great. Not because you're perfect. Because you care."

Aazar blinked, feeling her eyes sting.

"I don't know if I deserve this kind of faith from everyone," she whispered.

"You don't have to deserve it," KJ said gently, reaching out to take her hand. "Just receive it."

She met his gaze, her heart a wild thing, full and breaking all at once. "I do."

"Then let's get through this," he said, the faintest smile pulling at his lips.

Aazar nodded.

From inside the house, the soft hum of energy pulsed: Benji had finally managed to hold his power steady.

Aazar smiled.

The house wasn't perfect. Neither were they.

But it was enough.

The phone buzzed in Aazar's pocket, the sound jarring in the stillness of the back porch. She glanced at the screen, her chest tightening when she saw Caleb's name flash across it. The weight of the conversation she knew was coming pressed down on her, but she answered anyway, the familiar buzz of his voice echoing in her ear almost like a warning.

"Aazar," Caleb said, his voice sharp but tired. "I need you."

Aazar swallowed, her heart pounding against her ribs. She looked at the open sky, the wind tugging at her hair, and tried to steady herself. Her fingers tightened around the phone, and for a moment, she almost couldn't find the words.

"I can't do this anymore, Caleb," she said, the words slipping out before she could stop them.

There was a pause on the other end of the line, a silence that made the space between them feel miles apart. She could practically hear him processing it, his mind whirring with confusion.

"You can't do what?" Caleb asked, disbelief threading through his voice. "Aazar, we're so close to the end."

"I know," she said quietly, squeezing her eyes shut. "But it's too much. I can't keep this up and keep living my regular life."

Caleb was quiet again, but this time, she heard a faint crackling on the line, like he was pacing. His sigh was heavy.

"Aazar, don't do this," he said, his voice breaking just a little. "We've been through hell, but...but..."

She closed her eyes tighter, a lump rising in her throat. She could feel her pulse in her ears, the old wounds still fresh, still open. She hoped he wouldn't ask anymore questions.

"I just can't work for you anymore. I can't be this person. I've done enough violent work."

"Is this about the kiss?"

"No, no. I just need more time with my friends."

There was a long pause, the kind that stretched between breaths. Aazar bit down on her lip, feeling the weight of every moment in the silence.

"You're making a mistake, Aazar," he said, quieter now. "But if that's what you need... I won't force you."

"I'm sorry," she whispered, her voice breaking. "I really am. But I need to let go."

There was a long exhale from Caleb, followed by the sound of him shifting, like he was sitting down, his frustration palpable even from miles away. There was a long, drawn-out silence. Then the sharp click of the line as he hung up.

Aazar stared at the screen for a long moment, her heart hammering in her chest. She didn't know if Caleb was simply mad or if he had an idea of her plan.

The sun was setting in the distance, the sky burning with colors that felt too alive for her. She let the phone fall from her hand, her fingers trembling, and finally allowed herself to breathe.

Sprung

Aazar stood at the back entrance of the rehabilitation facility, her pulse thundering in her chest. This was the place: the one she'd seen with her own eyes, where human minds were mined and left hollow, reduced to nothing. She had no idea if it was unguarded. There was no guarantee, but there was no choice anymore. The time for planning, for waiting, was over. They had come this far, and they had to move now.

Beside her, Monica's expression darkened, her eyes narrowed. "Something feels wrong."

Flenoid crouched on Aazar's other side, his usual composure unshaken. "We've planned for every possibility."

Monica didn't take her eyes off the facility. "It still feels like a trap."

"Okay," Aazar said. "We'll all go in together."

But they moved anyway, the silence of the night hanging heavy around them. The team spread into position as they reached the door. Simon began bending the light around them, cloaking their presence. KJ walked beside Aazar, his fingers sparking with the faintest crackle of electricity, the tension in his body betraying his calm exterior. Flenoid, always vigilant, took up the rear, his eyes scanning their flank. Logan, confined to a brace after the last mission, stayed behind at the temporary base with a small group of newer recruits.

Aazar pressed her palm against the cold, smooth surface of the door, the metal chilling against her skin. She didn't hesitate before she used her fire to melt the door handle, sending a hiss of steam into the air. "Let's go," she said, her voice steady.

Simon moved first, extending his hand and weaving light into an illusion. The air shimmered, distorting around them like water bending to some unseen force. One by one, the team slipped through the illusion, moving silently into the sterile interior.

The silence that greeted them inside felt wrong. Too quiet. No alarms blaring. No guards. It was almost… too easy.

That's when they saw him.

Standing in the center of the dimly lit corridor was Caleb. His posture was casual, too casual for the situation. His hands were tucked neatly in his pockets, his sharp suit and effortless grin completely out of place in the sterile, humming space.

"Surprise!" he said, amusement lacing his voice. "You didn't think we'd see this coming?"

Aazar's breath caught in her chest, her heart skipping a beat. "Where's Johnny?" she demanded, her voice sharp, the words coming out before she could fully think them through.

Caleb's smile didn't falter. He stood there, unbothered, like they were simply meeting for a casual conversation. "Oh, he's around," he said airily. "We didn't like how you just quit, Z. It hurt my feelings."

Monica's muscles tensed beside Aazar. "I told you this was a trap," she muttered, her voice low and steady, but there was an edge to it.

Caleb laughed, and it was a cold, mirthless sound that echoed in the sterile hallway.

Suddenly, the lights above them flickered: an almost imperceptible stutter, before the chaos erupted.

From hidden doors, the Legacy enforcers emerged. Their eyes gleamed with malice, their powers crackling in the air like a gathering storm. The hallway, once quiet and sterile, erupted into pandemonium. One of the enforcers, a tall, scarred man with dark eyes, aimed a bolt of raw kinetic force at a young girl in their crew, no older than fifteen. The blast shot forward with terrifying speed, too quick for the girl to dodge.

Flenoid moved before anyone else. He threw himself in front of the blast without hesitation, his hands raised to create a shield. The pulse of energy slammed into his protective barrier with a deafening crack. His shield shattered instantly under the immense pressure, but it slowed the impact enough to protect the girl. Flenoid was thrown backward, slamming hard into the floor. His body hit the ground with a sickening thud.

"No!" Monica screamed, her voice raw, frantic. She darted toward the fallen Flenoid, her eyes wide with panic.

Aazar's heart hammered as the hallway erupted in violence. The moment Flenoid was down, all semblance of strategy evaporated. Chaos consumed them.

Aazar surged forward. Her body became an inferno. Flames ignited along her arms, consuming her skin in rippling waves of fire. Her eyes blazed with red, and she moved with the fury of a storm. She slammed into the first Legacy enforcer in her path, a woman with silver hair and cruel eyes. Aazar's fist landed squarely in her chest, sending her flying back into a nearby wall with a crash.

Before she could even process her victory, Caleb's laugh cut through the madness.

"Coward!" Aazar shouted, her throat tight with anger. "Show yourself!"

Caleb's voice echoed from somewhere in the shadows, mocking, taunting. "Not cowardice, darling. Strategy."

Aazar growled in frustration, her hands crackling with power. She spotted him: just a flicker of movement in the dim light near a control panel. She charged, flames trailing in her wake, but Caleb was already gone, disappearing in another blur of super-speed.

"Damn it!" she cursed, pushing through the throng of enemies. The Legacy soldiers were closing in, but Aazar didn't stop. She fought with the intensity of someone who knew there was no time to lose.

KJ was beside her, electricity crackling around his fingers. His power was less controlled than usual, his movements sharp with tension. He slammed a fist into the wall, sending a surge of electricity into the exposed wiring. Sparks flew, and several of the enforcers froze, temporarily stunned by the blast.

Simon was quick on his feet, moving through the chaos with practiced ease. He threw out his hands, bending the light around them. The enforcers nearest him staggered back as they were blinded by a flash so bright it burned their retinas. The hall was lit up like daylight in the middle of a storm. Simon, undeterred by the chaos, whipped around to strike again, using his light manipulation to blind anyone who dared get too close.

Monica was a whirlwind of motion, shifting through the fight with her usual grace. She grabbed the young girl Flenoid had saved and hauled her toward the safety of a nearby alcove. Monica didn't hesitate, her focus never wavering as she made sure the girl was out of the line of fire.

Aazar's focus never strayed from Caleb. She had to find him. She had to finish this.

"Where are you hiding, Caleb?!" she screamed, her voice raw.

Then, without warning, the hallway lights went out completely. Total darkness swallowed them, and Aazar's heart skipped a beat. Panic surged, but she shoved it aside. She couldn't afford to panic now. She summoned more fire, the heat around her growing intense enough to cut through the darkness like a blade.

The enforcers were relentless. One launched himself toward Aazar, his eyes glowing with an electric blue aura, his fist crackling with raw power. He slammed into her with the force of a freight train, knocking the breath from her lungs. Aazar grunted, but her fire flared, sending the enforcer stumbling backward, his face scorched and his armor charred.

She twisted around just in time to see KJ being overrun by two more enforcers. His electricity was sparking out of control, and the enforcers were closing in on him.

Without thinking, Aazar threw herself into the fray, pushing past the chaos. She reached KJ just as one of the enforcers swung a blade toward his exposed side. Aazar slammed her hand into the enforcer's chest, flames engulfing him in an instant. He screamed in pain, but Aazar didn't stop. She drove him back with a forceful kick, sending him crashing into the opposite wall.

"Get up!" she shouted at KJ, her voice thick with adrenaline.

KJ nodded, his breath ragged but his will unwavering. He scrambled to his feet, electricity once again arcing from his fingertips. The two enforcers who'd been circling him fell back, momentarily stunned by the shock wave of energy KJ sent out.

Aazar's eyes scanned the battlefield. It was chaos: there was no rhyme or reason to it now. The fight raged on around them, but her mind stayed fixed on one goal: finish the mission. Destroy the machine.

"Monica, come with me!" Aazar ordered, her voice ringing with command. "We need to get eyes on that machine!"

KJ, ever loyal, moved to her side as she reached the next door. With a fiery strike, Aazar burned through the door's lock, sending it flying open. Beyond it was the laboratory hall, its walls gleaming white and pristine. The hum of the machine was louder here, lower, guttural: like something breathing in its sleep.

Aazar's steps slowed as she crossed the threshold into the lab, her senses on high alert. The space was far cleaner than the chaos of the upper levels. The walls were bright, sterile: clinical. There was no disorder, no signs of panic. It looked like a hospital. Purposeful. Sanitized.

The machine stood in the center of the room, its sleek, silver limbs arching outward like ribs, curving over the dozens of beds beneath it. And in those beds… people. Hundreds of them. They lay still, their bodies connected to the machine with a network of wires fed into the backs of their necks, down their spines, across their temples. Their eyes flickered, their pupils moving erratically under closed lids, like they were dreaming. But there was no rhythm to it. No pulse. Just flickers. Static.

Aazar took a tentative step forward, her breath shallow as she moved closer to the nearest bed. The figure in the bed was thin, too thin, his skin pale and stretched tight over the bones. Mid-forties, maybe older. His face was worn, like grief had hollowed him out from the inside. The monitors beeped steadily around him, but it was the faintest detail: something about his brow, his expression, that caught her attention.

She paused, her stomach lurching in disbelief.

Her breath caught in her throat, and her voice, when it came, was barely a whisper. "Dad?"

Disappearing Act

Her gaze drifted across the room, her steps tentative, as if the very air in the room was charged with something she couldn't name.

Another bed. A woman with long black hair, grayer now than it had been in her memory, but unmistakable. Her mother.

Aazar's knees buckled, the shock of recognition threatening to drown her. She gripped the side of the machine to stay upright, her breathing shallow. She couldn't tear her eyes away from the figure in the bed.

"No," she whispered. "No, it can't be."

The man in the bed stirred. His eyes cracked open, glinting weakly in the dim light.

"…Aazar?"

Her heart skipped. His voice was weak, but it was unmistakably his. Raspy and sunken, but real.

"Dad?" she choked out, her voice breaking on the word.

His fingers twitched against the sheet, as if trying to reach for her. Aazar rushed to his side, kneeling beside the bed.

"I thought: I thought you were dead," he rasped, his voice a hoarse whisper. He coughed, a dry, labored sound, the effort leaving him pale. "We… we ran. We didn't know what else to do."

Aazar's chest constricted. She clenched her jaw, fighting the sting of old wounds. "You didn't even try to find me."

"I was scared," he said, his eyes fluttering closed. "We both were. You had powers… we didn't understand. People started watching us."

His breathing slowed, his words becoming more fragmented as he spoke, a fading light flickering out.

"We came here… hoping for a reset. They told us this machine… could give us peace."

Aazar's vision blurred, her hand trembling as it hovered over his. Her father had been larger than life to her, a constant presence, a rock. And now, seeing him so shriveled and frail in that hospital bed, it was too much to bear.

He opened his eyes one last time, the flicker of recognition there, but also something else: a deep sadness. "I'm sorry, baby. We were wrong."

And then, he was gone.

No beep. No monitor flat-lining. Just… stillness. A profound silence that swallowed the room whole.

Aazar stared, unable to move, the weight of loss settling on her chest like a boulder. The world around her seemed to quiet, as if the moment itself held its breath. She couldn't cry out. She couldn't scream. She simply watched, paralyzed, as the life drained from the man she had once loved more than anything.

Her eyes flicked toward her mother's bed. The woman who had given her life, who had been there through it all, was lying motionless. Her lips were slightly parted, her hands limp by her sides. For a moment, Aazar could almost pretend that she was simply sleeping, that all the years of distance, of unanswered questions, were some twisted dream.

"Mom?" she whispered, but her mother didn't answer.

Aazar reached out with trembling hands, brushing a strand of hair from her mother's face. It was something she hadn't done in years, something she hadn't thought about since she was a little girl. She remembered the quiet moments when her mother would cry in the kitchen, thinking no one could see her. Aazar had been too young then to understand the sorrow that ran so deep in the woman who had always seemed so strong.

Now, Aazar understood it all too well.

She stepped around the machine, her fingers hovering near the neural feed. A single plug protruded from the base of her mother's skull. Her breath hitched as she glanced at the cold, metal contraption: the very thing that had taken so much from her. And in that moment, the reality of what this place had done to them, to everyone, crashed down on her.

"I'm sorry," she whispered, the words barely a breath as she yanked the plug free.

The machine whined in protest, the sound screeching through the sterile silence. Her mother's body jerked once, the jolt sharp and unnatural. Then, just as quickly, it settled back into the stillness.

And Aazar… sank.

She crumpled to the floor, her knees drawn to her chest as she folded inward. There were no cries of anguish, no desperate wails. Just a quiet trembling, a surrender to the pain that had been buried deep inside her for so long.

Because there wasn't time for a breakdown. There wasn't space for weakness. But in that moment, just for a moment, Aazar let herself fall apart: just enough to mourn the people she'd lost long before they ever stepped into that machine.

Monica burst into the room, the door slamming behind her with a force that echoed through the sterile walls. Her eyes were wide with fear, her breath ragged as she took in the scene before her. When her gaze landed on Aazar, trembling on the floor, the fear turned to confusion.

"Aazar?" Monica's voice cracked. "What's wrong?"

Aazar quickly wiped her face, though it did little to hide the wetness in her eyes. "Nothing. It's just… so sad."

She stood slowly, her legs unsteady beneath her. She walked toward the Consciousness Extractor, the sight of it making her stomach twist with disgust. The machine was still feeding, still pulsing with life: her parents' lives: trapped within it.

Monica stood frozen at the main console, her hands hovering over the controls. The tension in the room was thick, both of them staring at the machine that had stolen everything from them.

"Monica," Aazar said softly, her voice barely a whisper. "We have to shut it down."

But Monica didn't move. She couldn't.

Aazar stepped closer, her heart pounding as the screens flickered with activity. Waves of data, memory maps, brain signatures. It was all laid out before them. Lines of code translating into flashing, looping images of lives that had once been real.

A child's laughter. A scream. A kiss. A last breath.

And Monica was staring at all of it. "These are precious," she whispered, her voice strained.

Aazar frowned. "What?"

Monica's hand trembled. "It's their whole lives. They're here. I can see them. They're not gone. Destroying this machine means losing everything."

Aazar's gaze moved to the screen. Dozens: no, hundreds: of files scrolled past, each labeled with dates and names. Each file a person, a life, a memory. Aazar's heart twisted with grief for them all, for the people they had lost and the people who would never be free.

"We don't have time," Aazar said, her voice steady but taut with urgency. She placed a hand on Monica's shoulder, grounding her. "You can't make it right. Just shut it down so no one else gets trapped here."

Monica hesitated, her fingers hovering over the console as if torn between what was right and what felt impossible. Then, with a deep, shaky breath, she reached out and began typing. The machine groaned in protest, its lights flickering red, a warning sign that echoed through the sterile hall.

Somewhere in the distance, sirens wailed.

Aazar turned one last time to her parents. Her father's chest had stopped rising. Her mother was still, too peaceful for this world. She let her eyes linger for only a moment, then looked away before she could change her mind.

Then, the sound she dreaded most: clapping.

"Touching," Johnny's voice echoed from the doorway, his tone laced with cruel amusement. He entered the room with a dozen psychic Variants flanking him, their eyes glowing faint violet. "Truly. You always had a flair for drama, Aazar."

Aazar's muscles tensed. She stepped forward, Monica instinctively pulling back to the wall.

"You're too late," Aazar said, her voice low but filled with defiance.

Johnny smiled, his grin sharp and mocking. "I don't think so," he replied, stepping over a fallen body with casual ease. "The machine still works. And you've made eliminating you so much easier by gathering your little rebellion all in one place."

He placed his hand against his head and stared into Aazar's eyes. The air around them thick with invisible pressure. Aazar could feel the weight of it pressing down on her chest, the pull of his powers.

She readied herself, fire already beginning to build along her fingertips. Her heart was pounding, but she wasn't going to back down.

We can't win, she heard herself think, *we should just give up.*

"Get out of my head!" she screamed.

Monica looked confused. "What's going on? What is he doing?"

We should just kill ourselves, Aazar heard herself think.

"Stop!"

Then, the impossible happened.

"GET AWAY FROM HER!"

Hugo.

He emerged from the shadows, bloodied, bruised, but alive. He charged toward Johnny with a frozen blade made of concentrated water. Johnny turned, surprised, and for just a split second, he hesitated.

It was enough.

Hugo plunged the frozen blade into Johnny's chest with a brutal strike. The psychic's body jerked, his eyes wide with shock. His mouth opened, but no words came. Slowly, painfully, he collapsed to the floor, his life draining out of him.

The machine screamed in protest, red lights strobing wildly.

"It's overloading," Monica cried, panic creeping into her voice. "We have to leave!"

"Where's Caleb?!" Aazar shouted, the urgency of the moment overwhelming her.

"Gone," Flenoid said, limping in from the side hall, his blood-soaked sleeve evidence of the battle. "He ran."

Aazar gave one final, lingering look at her parents: at the people she had loved, at the people she had lost: before turning away.

"EVERYONE OUT!" she yelled.

The team fled through the collapsing halls, the heat rising, smoke curling through the air, memories swirling in the chaos. They were running, but there were some things you could never outrun.

Betrayal

Smoke hung thick in the air like fog: only sharper, more pungent, clinging to the wreckage around them. The halls of the rehabilitation center still trembled with the echoes of destruction. Aazar stepped out first, the soles of her boots crunching against broken glass and melted wires beneath her. Every step felt heavier than the last. Monica followed closely, her face pale and unreadable, eyes rimmed red: not from the smoke, but from the horror she had just witnessed. The things she had seen, the things she'd never forget.

Neither of them spoke. The silence stretched between them, suffocating.

The doors behind them sealed shut with a final, mechanical hiss, trapping the wreckage of the consciousness machine and the bodies of those who had once been tethered to it. Aazar didn't dare look back. She knew that if she did, she might crumble: she wasn't sure she could keep walking forward.

Avery was waiting.

He stood near the staging bay, flanked by half a dozen Order members, their breath still heavy from the earlier fight. His suit was torn, bloodstained at the collar, but he stood tall, commanding. His arms were folded across his chest, and the confidence in his eyes was unmistakable.

"While we're all congratulating ourselves," Avery began, his voice calm, self-assured, "I think it's time someone takes real control of what's left of this region. The Legacy strongholds are vulnerable. Their infrastructure is rattled. We need order: and leadership. I'm prepared to claim the California Islands in the name of the reformed Order."

Aazar froze. The words hung in the air like a threat. Monica stepped closer, her fingers twitching with residual power, her stance defensive.

"You're what?" Aazar asked, her voice low but sharp. Flenoid had been correct.

Avery gestured calmly to the chaos surrounding them: broken walls, unconscious bodies, flashing alarms. "They need stability. A presence. Someone who isn't afraid to take control when the fire clears. You said it yourself, Aazar. They need someone to lead."

Aazar stepped forward, her gaze steady, unwavering. "You don't get to decide that."

Avery's eyes flashed with something dark, his jaw tightening. "Then who does? You?"

Before Aazar could respond, a loud crack echoed from the far corridor. She heard Todd scream. "You did this!"

Aazar turned.

Todd stood in the corridor, half-lit by emergency strobes, his face streaked with ash and blood that wasn't all his. His eyes glowed too bright, too focused, like something inside him had finally snapped into place.

KJ came up behind him. Electricity crawled across his arms in restless arcs, snapping against the walls.

"No," KJ said. "You did."

"You didn't hesitate to ditch me," Todd replied.

Aazar stepped between them without thinking.

"Stop," she said. "Both of you. This place is coming down."

Neither of them listened.

"You left me," Todd said, his voice steady in a way that terrified her. "You decided I was already lost."

"I left because I was watching you disappear," KJ snapped. "Because staying meant pretending this was okay."

Aazar lifted her hands, heat humming beneath her skin. "This isn't the time. We move together, or we don't move at all."

Todd's eyes flicked to her. Something sharp flashed there: resentment, maybe jealousy.

"You're always in the way."

"I'm trying to keep you alive." She said fiercely.

Todd laughed once. "Then you're failing."

The floor shuddered violently. Concrete groaned overhead.

"Look at me," Aazar said, stepping closer to Todd. Carefully, she reached out emotionally. She felt it instantly: the fracture, the pressure, the way Todd was holding himself together by momentum alone.

"This ends here," she said. "We survive this."

Todd's gaze slid past her, locking back onto KJ.

"You don't get to decide that."

He lunged.

KJ moved at the same time.

They collided hard, slamming into the wall. Glass exploded. Electricity detonated down the corridor, lights bursting overhead.

"STOP!" Aazar screamed.

She threw a wave of heat between them—not flame, just force. Enough to stagger them apart.

For half a second, it worked.

KJ looked at her, chest heaving. Todd wiped blood from his mouth, his eyes blazing brighter.

"You're afraid," Todd said. "Both of you."

Aazar shook her head. "I'm afraid of losing you."

Todd's smile sharpened. "Then you already have."

His thoughts slammed outward, raw and uncontrolled. Aazar gasped as the psychic backlash hit her, emotions spiking painfully through her chest. KJ cried out, electricity exploding from his body in response.

The corridor dissolved into chaos.

Aazar dropped to one knee, fire flaring instinctively around her hands. She forced it down, teeth clenched, lungs burning.

"KJ—don't—!" she shouted.

It was already too late.

They charged each other again. Power collided violently, thunder and sparks and screaming metal. The building protested, structural alarms shrieking louder as walls cracked and debris rained down.

Aazar pushed herself to her feet, fire trembling along her arms.

"ENOUGH!" she screamed, unleashing a blast of heat between them—blinding, searing, forcing space.

The explosion threw them apart.

Smoke swallowed the corridor.

Todd staggered but stayed upright. KJ slammed into the wall, electricity crackling uselessly around him.

Aazar stood between them, shaking, soot and tears streaking her face.

"Please," she said hoarsely. "Not like this."

Todd looked at her. Then his expression closed.

"You can't save everyone," he said quietly.

Another explosion rocked the building, close enough to knock her sideways.

Their powers flared: wild and volatile. Sparks rained down from the ceiling as KJ unleashed a wave of electricity that barely missed Todd's shoulder. Todd ducked low, his telepathy visibly shaking KJ's concentration, amplifying the tension. Their fight was raw, personal, carried the weight of years unspoken, years broken.

Avery moved beside Aazar, watching the fight with cold fascination. "They'll kill each other."

"Then stop them," Aazar hissed, her voice venomous.

Avery shrugged. "That isn't my responsibility."

Aazar glared at him before turning to Monica. "Get the remaining Variants out to the rendezvous area."

Monica nodded and sprinted toward the exit.

The smoke hadn't cleared. It clung to the fractured night air like grief made visible. Aazar stood at the edge of the courtyard, her chest heaving, the scent of scorched stone and blood clinging to her skin. Her arms ached, her mind buzzing with too many voices: some of them real, some just memories: painful, all of them.

Suddenly, she noticed Avery had disappeared from her side. Before she could speak again, KJ grabbed her arm.

"Go."

She stared at him. "What?"

He didn't look away from Todd. His eyes were steady now—resolved in a way that frightened her more than panic ever had.

"Go find Avery," KJ said. "He's still in this building."

"KJ—"

"I can handle this," he said, low and final. "I need to."

Electricity tightened around his fist: controlled this time, contained.

Her heart pounded painfully. "You don't have to do this alone."

He finally looked at her.

"I do," he said softly. "Please."

Todd watched them, his expression unreadable.

The building groaned again, warning of imminent danger.

Aazar swallowed hard and nodded. She squeezed KJ's arm once.

"Don't die," she whispered.

He gave a humorless half-smile. "I'll try."

She turned and ran, fire guiding her through smoke and falling debris.

Behind her, electricity surged.

Todd stepped forward.

"This ends now," he said.

And as the corridor erupted in light and thunder, Aazar ran toward the war room, never knowing that the choice she had just honored would fracture everything that came next. She didn't know what the future of the California Islands looked like, but she knew one thing for sure: It wouldn't belong to Avery.

Avery stood at the center of the ruined war room, blood staining his jacket, his eyes wild with power. He looked older and grimmer, or maybe she was finally seeing him for what he truly was.

He looked at her and smiled, the grin stretching wide. "We did it! We stopped them! Now we can shape this world however we want it."

Aazar felt the flames tickle her fingers. He glanced down at them, and his smile faltered.

"We could've ruled together. Rebuilt The Order. Brought the Legacies to their knees. But you always have to be the martyr. You have to be the hero."

Aazar's voice came out hoarse, steady despite the raw emotion coiling inside her. "I never wanted to rule. I just wanted to be free."

Avery laughed, bitter and raw. "There is no freedom. Only power. You either take it, or you are crushed by it."

He raised his hand, and Aazar felt her ribs seize, the telekinetic grip tightening around her body. She gasped, her breath caught in the pressure. He had always had that ability: the power to take control of her, to manipulate her. It had always been his way. But now, she wouldn't let him win.

Aazar's body erupted in flames, a searing golden light that crackled with pure emotion. She slammed herself against his hold, pushing against his telekinesis with every ounce of strength she had. Fire met telekinesis. Their powers clashed violently, an explosion of raw, unrestrained energy that cracked through the stone floor beneath them.

Aazar flamed out in a burst that scorched the walls, sending waves of heat that shook the room, but Avery flung her back. She hit a broken table, the impact rattling her bones, but she didn't stop. She got up harder, faster. Her fury was a river, unstoppable, and it flowed through her like a fire that could never be extinguished.

Her heart thudded in her chest. She threw a fireball at him, watching as it twisted mid-air and exploded at his feet, knocking him off balance. The room shook with the impact, but Avery recovered instantly. His face twisted with fury as he sent shards of metal flying toward her, sharp and unrelenting. She melted them mid-air, her flames a barrier between them.

But it wasn't enough. She needed to do more. She needed to end this.

Avery lifted her again with his mind, slamming her against the far wall. The blow knocked the air out of her lungs. Her vision blurred, and her head spun. His power gripped her ribs, squeezing, crushing her from the inside out.

"You were always going to betray me," he snarled, his voice thick with venom. "You've always been the one to run away."

Aazar coughed, blood filling her mouth. She fought to breathe, to stay focused. And then, with every last ounce of strength, she ignited once more.

Her body flared with a golden, blinding light: her entire being igniting, burning brighter than ever before. It was more than just fire. It was everything. Every pain. Every loss. Every betrayal. It was the culmination of years of grief, anger, and heartbreak.

Avery shielded his eyes, but it didn't stop her. It wasn't enough to blind him: it was enough to burn him. She dropped to the floor, rolled, and threw herself at him. This time, she didn't hold back. This time, there was nothing left to lose.

She pressed her palm to his chest: skin to skin.

The emotion flooded him, rushing through his body. All of it. Years of rage, of shame, of guilt. Every death she carried, every friend she had failed. The pain of losing herself: her mother, Norma, everything she had kept buried for so long.

Avery screamed, his body jerking with the force of it. He tried to fight it: tried to push her away, but she held on, refusing to let go. Her flames seared through him, not just physically, but emotionally, every ounce of her suffering pouring into him. She wanted him to feel it. She wanted him to understand.

"Let me go," she whispered, her voice breaking.

The explosion of energy sent them both flying. The force was so intense that it shook the room, sending debris scattering in all directions.

When the dust settled, Aazar lay gasping for breath, her body trembling from the effort. Her vision swam. Every muscle in her body screamed with exhaustion. But she didn't care.

Avery didn't get up.

His chest was still. His face twisted in something like sorrow, or maybe it was just the way the light hit him. He looked so small now. So empty.

KJ stumbled into the room, one eye nearly swollen shut. Todd was behind him, defeated but breathing, crumpled against the wall, unconscious.

Aazar didn't speak. She couldn't. There were no words left. Not for him. Not for any of this.

KJ looked at her, then at Avery. His shoulders dropped, a deep sigh escaping his lips as he took in the finality of it all.

"It's over," he said, his voice thick with something Aazar couldn't quite place.

But it didn't feel like a victory. Not when everything had already been lost. Not when they had all paid such a steep price. Aazar was surprised when the tears began to fall from her eyes.

Simon and Monica arrived, guiding more of their people into the room. No one cheered. No one clapped. The air was thick with grief. With loss. With everything they had fought for slipping through their fingers like sand.

Aazar looked down at her hands. They were still shaking.

"He thought I was the threat," she murmured, her voice barely audible.

KJ nodded slowly, his eyes filled with something more than just sadness. "You were."

And for once, she didn't flinch at the word.

Outside, the sky began to lighten, the first light of dawn creeping over the horizon. A new day. But there was no joy in it. Only the quiet, heavy certainty that the world they had fought for was now forever changed.

New Order

The machine was gone.

The silence it left behind felt too loud, like a weight pressing against the world. It was the kind of stillness that made everything seem heavier, more uncertain, like the earth was holding its breath.

Aazar stood near the wreckage, smoke curling around her ankles like ghosts. The core had burned out quickly, a final hiss of light and heat as Monica's hand pressed the shutdown command. The machine's quiet death rippled through the facility, the way a held breath is finally exhaled: relieved but suffocating. The walls, once pulsing with stolen thoughts, now stood still. Empty. Silent.

No more data. No more screams locked in wires.

Simon helped Monica to her feet. She was pale, her lips trembling, her body shaking with exhaustion. But she was still standing, her resolve unbroken. Aazar met her eyes, offering a silent nod. Monica nodded back, her gaze steady but haunted.

Outside, the chaos was dying down. Some of the younger Variants huddled in corners, dazed, their bodies trembling from the aftermath. Others stood over the unconscious bodies of the Legacy guards who hadn't fled with Caleb. The war wasn't over, not really. But the heart of it: the machine that had fed on human thought like a parasite: was finally gone. And that was something.

Flenoid leaned against the side of the wall, his breathing shallow, his robes torn. His left shoulder hung at an odd angle, but when Aazar approached, he smiled, his expression still defiant, even through the pain.

"We did it," he said, his voice ragged.

"Not without cost," Aazar replied quietly, her gaze drifting over the wreckage.

"Victory never comes free," Flenoid muttered, straightening with a wince.

Aazar's eyes scanned the facility, taking in the fractured remains of what had once been a prison disguised as a solution. Maybe that was what most of their world had become: illusions pretending to be answers. But this time, they had torn one down.

Flenoid winced as he straightened, his breath shallow. "I won't be leading anymore. Not in the way they need."

She nodded slowly, understanding what he meant. "Then who?"

Simon approached, his hand clasped firmly around Monica's. He looked nervous, but resolute, as if this moment was something he had already decided. Monica, still silent, stood tall at his side, her presence calm but unyielding.

"Them," Flenoid said simply, his voice steady. "They'll lead the new Order."

Aazar's gaze shifted to Simon and Monica. She watched as Simon squeezed Monica's hand, his fingers tight with a quiet strength. And Monica... For all her shadows, she had a wisdom about her, a burden carried in the memories of others.

Aazar studied them both. "Are you ready for that?" she asked, her voice a mixture of challenge and understanding.

Monica nodded, her expression hardening. "We have to be."

Simon smiled faintly, the corners of his lips barely lifting. "We won't make the same mistakes."

Aazar met their gaze for a moment, her eyes searching. She saw the resolve in them, the shared weight of responsibility. For the first time, she allowed herself a small, hesitant smile. "See that you don't."

Later, in the ruined courtyard, KJ stood with Todd.

The air between them was fragile, tense, like it might shatter at any moment.

Todd's eyes were bloodshot, his shirt torn, his hands curled into fists. But he wasn't fighting anymore. Not physically. Just standing there, as if waiting for something: anything: to make sense.

"So this is it," Todd said, his voice thick with bitterness. "You get to be the better brother. The hero."

KJ shook his head slowly, the weight of the words sinking into him. "No heroes left, Todd. Just survivors."

Todd let out a bitter laugh, the sound hollow. "I killed for him. Followed every order. And when I finally looked up… everything I believed in was gone."

KJ stepped closer, his voice low, but firm. "It doesn't have to haunt you."

Todd looked at him, his eyes shimmering with something KJ couldn't quite read: regret, perhaps. Or hope.

"Monica offered to erase everything," Todd said quietly, almost as if admitting something to himself. "The memories. The pain. The things I did."

KJ inhaled sharply, the thought of losing Todd, of losing everything, gnawing at him. "And you're going to let her?"

Todd's gaze dropped to the ground, his voice barely a whisper. "I don't want to live with it anymore. I can't forgive myself. But maybe I can start over."

There was silence between them. KJ's heart ached for his brother: for the man who had done unspeakable things, but had never truly wanted to.

"If you do this…" KJ began, voice soft but filled with an unspoken promise, "I'll take care of you. I'll be there when you wake up. I won't leave you again."

Todd's breath hitched. His eyes flickered up to meet KJ's.

"You'd do that?" Todd asked, disbelief in his voice.

KJ nodded, his jaw tightening. "You're my brother," he said firmly. "No matter what version of you remembers me."

Todd sat down heavily on the edge of a stone bench, his shoulders slumped under the weight of the decision he was about to make. "Then I guess… it's time."

KJ nodded, reaching for his comm. "I'll call Monica."

When the sun rose the next day, the world hadn't changed.

But they had.

Monica sat beside Todd, her presence a calm anchor as his memories began to fade. Flenoid, wrapped in fresh bandages, meditated by the fire, his posture as steady as ever.

Aazar closed her eyes, taking a deep breath.

She had fought, bled, and burned for this moment, but it had cost her pieces she couldn't get back. She had lost so much: pieces of herself, of her family, of people who had meant everything. But maybe that was okay. Maybe that was what the fight was about.

The Order was reborn.

And something new was beginning. Even if she wasn't sure what came next.

Begin at the Close

The sun was just beginning to rise over the California Islands, brushing soft gold across the hills and cliffs, gilding the land that had soaked so much blood, so much fire. The land that had witnessed so many battles, so many losses. Aazar stood at the edge of the dirt road behind the house: the one they'd rebuilt three times since they arrived: a single bag slung over her shoulder. Her boots were still dusty from the night before, worn and weathered, like the rest of her. Her coat still smelled of smoke, a reminder of the fire that had claimed so much and yet left her standing.

She didn't turn when the car door creaked open behind her.

"So this is it?" KJ asked quietly, his voice carrying the weight of something unsaid. Something that hung in the air between them, thick with the unspoken past.

Aazar didn't answer right away. She just nodded once, her head lowering slightly as if the simple act of agreeing was too much to say aloud.

KJ took a slow step toward her, his boots crunching the dirt beneath his feet. His hands were shoved deep in his jacket pockets, his expression unreadable, like a mask he'd worn so long it had become his face. She could see the tension in his shoulders, the way his body was coiled tight, like he was waiting for something to break.

"You could stay," he said, his voice softer this time, as though he was offering her a way out. A way to stay in the world they had built: together.

"I know," she whispered, but the words felt too heavy to truly explain. She had known all along. Staying had never been an option. Not now.

Silence fell between them, thick and heavy, like a gentle mist settling in the space between their hearts. It wasn't awkward, not in the way words can be. It wasn't angry or resentful. It was simply full. Full of everything they had been to each other, everything they had lost, everything they had yet to understand.

"You did it," KJ said finally, his voice thick with something she couldn't quite place. "We survived."

Aazar's lips curved into a faint, almost imperceptible smile. "We did," she agreed. "And now you have to build something better."

KJ swallowed, his jaw tight. The muscles in his face shifted slightly, but he didn't say anything for a long moment. The weight of her words hung between them, and she knew he understood, even if he didn't want to.

"You don't have to do this alone," he said quietly. It wasn't a plea. It wasn't a demand. It was an offering, the kind only people who truly know each other can make.

Aazar turned to face him, her eyes soft, but steady. She could feel the weight of everything he wanted to say, but she knew it was time for her to go. Her voice was a low murmur, but firm. "I do. Not forever. But for now."

KJ nodded slowly, his face unreadable. But the muscle in his jaw twitched, a flicker of emotion passing through him before he masked it again.

Aazar stepped closer, the space between them so small now, just a breath away.

She reached for his hand, and after a moment of hesitation, he let her take it. His fingers were warm against hers, and for a moment, it felt like nothing had changed. But everything had.

"You were the best part of this," she said softly. Her voice trembled slightly, but she didn't look away. "Even when I couldn't admit it. Even when I pushed you away."

KJ blinked quickly, his eyes glossing over for just a moment. He didn't know how to respond to that. Neither of them did.

"Where will you go?" he asked, his voice barely above a whisper.

Aazar turned her gaze to the horizon, the faint light of the morning touching the tips of the hills. "Somewhere quiet. Somewhere untouched."

He nodded, but didn't speak again. The weight of their history settled between them like an anchor, keeping them both tethered to this moment. The unspoken words: everything they had been through together: hung in the air, unresolved.

"Take care of Todd," she said, her voice firm, though there was a quiet plea beneath it. "He'll need you."

"I will," KJ promised, his voice steady, but the shadows of their past still clouding his words.

Aazar leaned forward and pressed a kiss to his cheek. It lingered for a second longer than it should have, a small comfort, a shared moment of something they would never get back. Then she stepped back, feeling the weight of her next steps.

"Tell the others thank you," she said quietly. "For believing in me. Even when I didn't deserve it."

KJ didn't promise to pass it on. He didn't need to. He just stood there, watching her as she walked away, his hands still clenched into fists at his sides. The air between them was charged, but he didn't call her back.

Aazar turned away and began walking down the dirt road, the sun rising higher in the sky behind her. The road turned to grass, and the grass gave way to a long stretch of open field. No structures. No voices. No commands. Just the hum of the earth beneath her feet and the wind tugging at her hair.

She dropped her bag near a patch of shade beneath an ancient tree, its branches heavy with age and wisdom. The wind whispered through the wildflowers, sweeping around her like a living thing, tugging at the edges of her coat.

She lowered herself into the grass, her knees folding beneath her as she sat. Her palms rested flat on her thighs, grounding her to the earth. Her eyes closed, and for the first time in a long time, she breathed deeply.

In.

And out.

And in again.

The wind danced through her hair, tugging gently at the strands. There were no voices in her head. No rage, no fire. No war waiting in the wings.

No responsibilities. Just breath. Just grass. Just sky.

She didn't know how long she sat there. Maybe hours. Maybe days. Maybe forever. Time felt distant, irrelevant. But in that moment, for the first time in as long as she could remember, Aazar felt it: Peace.

It filled her ribs, expanded behind her eyes, curling into the tips of her fingers. She could feel the quiet settling in her bones, the tension she hadn't realized was there slowly unraveling.

Aazar exhaled slowly, the sound lost in the soft rustling of the wind.

Finally.

She was free.

About the Author

E.C. Madrid is the author of *The Aazar Series*, a dystopian fantasy trilogy exploring power, memory, rebellion, and the cost of belonging. Her work centers morally complex characters navigating systems of control, where survival often demands uncomfortable choices and peace rarely looks like victory.

She is drawn to stories about found family, inner darkness, and the quiet strength it takes to walk away from power. When she isn't writing, E.C. Madrid is building a life rooted in self-reliance, land stewardship, and intentional community in the American Southwest.

Her novels include *The Flickers of Fall*, *Children of the Order*, and *Variant Rising*.

You can connect with me on:
- https://www.ec-madrid.com
- https://x.com/AuthorECMadrid

Also by E.C. Madrid

The Flickers of Fall

In a world where Variant powers mean control or exile, Aazar has only ever known how to survive. But when betrayal ignites a rebellion, she must choose between vengeance and something far more dangerous—hope. *The Flickers of Fall* is a gripping tale of found family, buried truths, and the fire it takes to rise.

Children of The Order

The Order promised purpose. What Aazar found was control. As old allies fracture and secrets surface, she must navigate the ruins of rebellion and the weight of leadership. *Children of the Order* is a haunting journey through loyalty, loss, and the quiet war between who you are and who you're told to be.